Stuffing my Stocking

Stuffing my Stocking

| Ali Whippe | Honey Cummings | Jean Bex | Leo Sparx |
| Mimi Francis | Shae Coon |

4 Horsemen
Publications, Inc.

Dedication

To All the Naughty & Nice Readers,

May you find just the right amount of holiday magic in this collection to make your season a little naughty and very nice!

XOXO
The Authors

Table of Contents

Dedication V

Naughty or Nice by Mimi Francis 1

Kissing in the Closet by Shae Coon 19

The Twinks and the Harnessmaker by Leo Sparx 50

Home Free by Jean Bex 67

Ring My Bells by Honey Cummings 83

The Holiday Switch by Ali Whippe 103

Naughty or Nice

Mimi Francis

I raked my nails down his back, my back arching as he slammed into me. I couldn't get him close enough. I wanted every inch of him; I wanted to feel his body melding with mine. A garbled cry erupted from my throat—part scream, part moan, and something that sounded vaguely like yes—as the orgasm built to its peak and exploded through me. He buried his face against the side of my neck as his body shuddered, his hips flexing as he came.

My thighs trembled—

The incessant buzz of my alarm clock interrupted the dream, dragging me out of orgasmic bliss into my dimly lit apartment. I'd tangled the sheets around my legs, and my pussy throbbed with an unfulfilled need. Dream sex wasn't as good as the real thing.

I rolled to my side and hit the button to turn off the alarm. I swiped a hand down my face and groaned aloud.

"I have got to get over my crush on Santa," I said to the empty room.

I hurried down the street, zipping my jacket closed as I went. The weather had finally turned, and the snow fell. It was about time. Christmas was a week away. Once again, I wished I'd checked the weather before leaving the house this morning for my waitressing job. I didn't have a hat, gloves, or scarf. If I had time during my break, I would buy a set before I left Fielding's department store for the night. It meant finally taking advantage of the temporary employee discount Mr. Fielding pestered me to use.

Fielding's was the only family-owned department store left in Lakeside. It took up an entire street corner and during the holiday season, it boasted one of the best Santa displays in the state of Montana. People came from as far away as Bozeman to see it. I'd taken a part-time job as one of Santa's elves for the season, hoping to get some extra money in my savings account. I needed every dime possible if I was going to start school at Lakeside University next year.

The department store was on the corner, the windows ablaze with Christmas lights and beautifully decorated trees. Through the glass, I saw Santa's Toyland and the line of children waiting to see Santa. It twisted its way through the roped off area, into the seasonal department, and ended near the toy department.

I'm going to be on my feet forever.

I made my way around the block to the back, yanked open the "Employees Only" door in the alley, and darted down the hall. I checked my watch. I was going to be late. I threw my coat in my locker, kicked off my tennis shoes, and grabbed my costume. I ducked into the bathroom and pulled off my clothes. I quickly put on the green velvet skirt and matching green and white striped top, cursing out loud when I realized I'd forgotten to grab my green tights off the bathroom counter at home. I'd have to go without.

I checked my costume in the mirror and sent up a prayer that the knee-length skirt covered my simple white panties and didn't show too much skin. Fortunately, the matching boots hit well mid-thigh. It would have to be enough.

Back in the employee locker room, I threw my clothes in my locker, slipped on the thigh-high green velvet boots, put on the pointy elf ears, and set the hat on my head. I gave myself a quick once over in the full-length mirror, popped a mint in my mouth, and headed down the hall.

"Mari!"

The sound of his voice sent chills down my spine. I sucked in a deep breath and turned around.

"Hi, Kane."

He sidled up to me and bumped my side with his elbow. "How's my favorite elf?"

"I'm good." I laughed, but it came out sounding like a choked gurgle or something. Every time I talked to Kane, I got tongue-tied and my face burned. This morning's dream certainly wouldn't help.

My inability to form a complete sentence faded a little when he put on the white beard, the white wig, and buttoned his red velvet jacket over the fat suit. At least then I wouldn't see the muscles rippling beneath his t-shirt, or his thick black hair, stylishly messy, like he'd done nothing more than push a hand through it after he got out of the shower.

Why did he have to be so attractive? I couldn't even pretend I hated him. My inner monologue worked overtime trying to convince me I really did hate him, but I didn't. In fact, I had a huge crush on Kane. On Santa.

We'd been doing the does-he-like-me-or-not dance for a couple of weeks, constantly flirting, eating together on our lunch break, grabbing a coffee before work if we had time. We'd even gone on a date, kind of. We met at Roselli's for pizza and beer a week ago. After dinner, Kane walked me home and kissed my cheek goodnight. While it was a good start, it wasn't exactly what I wanted.

I want to unwrap him like a Christmas present.

I opened my mouth to tell him that—or something less creepy—but Lily, our lithe young photographer, chose that moment to bounce down the hallway toward us, a huge grin on her face. She rubbed a hand over her short, pink hair and blew a matching pink bubble with the wad of ever-present gum in her mouth. She grinned.

"Hiya," she chirped. "You guys ready? I ran into the day shift Santa, and he said it's been insane."

"It's because Christmas is in a week," I grumbled. "Everybody waits until the last minute."

"A week?" Kane said. "I only get to hang out with you for another week?"

I blushed and shook my head. "Less. We close early on Christmas Eve and of course, we don't work Christmas Day, so…"

"So, I better make the most of the time we have left. Santa may not find an elf as cute as you, again." Kane plopped the hat on his head and winked at me. He adjusted his black leather belt and pushed back the curtain covering the door. Loud cheers, squeals, and cries of "Hi, Santa" filled the air. He raised a hand to wave and stepped into the limelight.

I exhaled slowly, willing my heart to stop racing. I'd had a crush on Kane since we first met in November. We sat together at orientation—or Santa class, as Kane called it—laughing and joking at the ridiculousness of taking a class to ask kids what they wanted for Christmas, hand them a candy cane, and snap a picture. The second Kane flashed me his toothy grin, his green eyes sparkling, I'd been gone. The man had been starring in my dreams ever since.

Lily poked me. "Mari, let's go."

"Sorry," I muttered. I took one last look at my elf costume and followed Kane—Santa—through the curtain.

I spent the next two hours helping kids climb on Santa's lap, holding crying babies, keeping the line moving, and handing out candy canes. I did my best to ignore Kane's fingers grazing my back when I stood beside him with a squirming kid, his low whispers of gratitude when I plucked an upset child from his lap, and the way his eyes traced the curves of my body. By the time I stepped through the curtain into the back hallway, I was sweating.

How am I supposed to last another four hours?

Rather than endure another awkward minute with Kane, I spent our break wandering around the department store with a cup of coffee from the in-store coffee shop. Being away from Kane didn't stop the daydreams, though. My brain conjured images of the two of us walking hand in hand through the store, Christmas shopping. He would laugh at my silly puns and kiss my cheek when we found the perfect gifts for our friends and family. Once we were home, laden with bags and gifts, we wouldn't even make it through the door before he was kissing me and tugging at my clothes...

"Mari!"

My cheeks burned and coffee sloshed over the side of my cup as I jumped. I swung around to see Lily giggling at me. "Hey, I've been looking everywhere for you. You're late. Kane's trying to hold off a herd of kids on his own."

"Shit. Shit. Sorry." I tossed my cup in the nearest trash can and followed her back to Santa's Toyland. I totally forgot to buy tights.

I grabbed my hat and ears from the table in the hall and quickly put them on before slipping through the curtain, a forced smile on my face. Relief washed over Kane's face when he saw me. I hurried to his side, grabbed the child clinging to his leg, plopped them in Kane's lap, took the leash for the dog from the frenzied parent, and sat down next to Kane. Thirty seconds later, Lily had snapped the picture and the family was on their way.

"Thanks for rescuing me," Kane whispered.

I shrugged. "What kind of elf would I be if I didn't help Santa?"

Kane chuckled. "One with crooked ears." He reached over and straightened my pointy ears, his fingers sliding down my cheek and gently caressing my neck for a split second before it was over, like a dream. Like one of my dreams.

"I... uh... I guess I'll get the next kid." I rose to my feet to get the next child in line, but Kane grabbed my hand, stopping me.

"Hey, do you want to go out later? When we get off work, I mean?"

My head bounced on my neck like a dashboard bobble head. "Yeah, yeah, sure. That, um, that sounds great."

I cleared my throat and swallowed past the lump rising in my throat. I kept the smile plastered on my face, clasped my hands together, and prayed he wouldn't notice my stuttered breathing. I resisted the urge to throw my arms around him and beg him to fuck me. Not really the spectacle Fielding's would want in their Santa display.

"Thanks for fixing my ears," I muttered. I spun around and practically pounced on the next family in line. Work would take my mind off the naughty thoughts racing through my head.

It worked for a while. I concentrated on the kids, the pets, their parents, and the grandparents. I handed out candy cane after candy cane and I smiled so widely I thought my face might split in half. When Lily finally put the "Gone to Make Toys" on Santa's seat, my cheeks and neck muscles ached.

I need a drink.

Lily vanished as soon as she put the sign up, leaving Kane and me in the Santa's Toyland display alone. I took a deep breath and began straightening the toys, adjusting the ornaments on the trees, and restocking the candy canes. I was lost in my own little world, cleaning, straightening, and thinking about Kane and our date. It startled me when the overhead lights went out, plunging us into semi-darkness. The only lights came from the giant Christmas tree beside Santa's makeshift house. A squeak left me, and I sank to the stairs at the foot of Santa's sleigh.

Kane emerged from the curtained area behind Santa's seat. "Are you okay?"

"Yeah, sorry." I pulled my hat and ears off and set them on the stage beside me. "I didn't realize how late it was."

"Late? This is late?"

"In Lakeside, a week before Christmas? Yes, this is late."

"They don't waste any time getting out of here, do they?" He checked his watch. "It's not even 10:30."

I shrugged. "Fielding's is a family store. Roll up the sidewalks and send everyone home at ten on the nose."

He laughed. "Except us?"

I giggled nervously. "The security guard is downstairs. He'll let us out when we're ready to go."

"He doesn't patrol the store?"

"Clyde? Um, no. Clyde's philosophy is to do as little work as possible. He comes in when the store closes, goes into the security office, makes himself some coffee, and turns on ESPN. He won't move unless he absolutely has to."

Kane chuckled under his breath. "Sounds like a cushy job. So, are we still on for that date? We could get dinner or something? Or is it too late? Is anything still open at almost eleven on a Friday night?"

I scrunched up my nose. "How long have you lived in Lakeside?"

"Only a couple of months. You?"

"Longer than I ever thought I'd be here." I ran my hands down the length of my green velvet skirt, straightening the wrinkles. "The Time Out Bar and Grill is still open. Let's go there."

Kane nodded. "Okay, sure. Let's finish cleaning up so we can go."

I muttered some incoherent agreement, snatched my hat and ears off the steps, slipped behind the curtain, and set them on the table. When I stepped back through the curtain, Kane was right there. He'd removed the beard and the fat stomach prosthetic, leaving him in the red jacket over a tight, white t-shirt, and the red velvet pants with the black belt. Startled, I took a step back and bumped into the fake wall next to the curtain covered door that served as our exit and entrance.

"Can I ask you something, Mari?"

"Sh...sure," I stammered.

"Do you like me?"

I nodded. "Of course, I do. You're a nice guy—"

"No, I mean, do you like me *like* me?" He stepped right into my personal space and put his hand on the wall above my head. He leaned close and the scent of leather and sandalwood filled my head. I licked my lips and nodded.

Kane ducked his head, caught my lips in his, and kissed me. Soft, sweet, tender. I sighed and leaned into him, my arms slipping around his neck and my body flush against his. When we broke apart, Kane smiled and brushed his knuckles down my cheek.

"You're the prettiest elf I've ever met." He tucked a strand of hair behind my ears. "I've been wanting to kiss you since the day I met you."

"I've been wanting you to kiss me since we met." I giggled. "That and a few other things."

"Oh yeah?"

I giggled again and nodded. I rested my forehead against Kane's chest, embarrassed that the words had left my mouth. I refused to look him in the eye.

*Why don't you just tell him you have sex dreams about him, Mari? Embarrass
yourself some more.*

Kane put his huge hands on my shoulders and kneaded the tense muscles.
"Maybe instead of going to dinner, we stay here."

"Here?" I giggled and looked up at him. "In Santa's workshop?"

Kane nodded. His green eyes held mine, something inexplicable passing
between us. "Let's talk about the 'other things' you mentioned."

I snorted. I couldn't help it. I shook my head. "Do you want me to die of
embarrassment?"

He leaned over me and shook his head. "No. I want to kiss you. I want
to touch you. I want to do those other things to you. Does that bother you?
Scare you?"

"N...no," I stammered.

"Let's make it a game," he suggested. "Santa and his favorite elf. What
do you say?"

I released the breath I'd been holding and nodded. Kane moved in close, his
fingers moving up and down my neck, shoulders, and back, tracing the length of
my spine. He pressed a kiss to the top of my head, and when I tipped my head
back to look at him, he took my chin in his hand and kissed me. I opened my
mouth to let his tongue slip past my teeth and into my mouth.

The thought flitted through my head that this might be a bad idea, a colos-
sally bad idea. We were still in the store where someone might find us. Clyde
could come around the corner, or one of the associates could still be in the store
and see us.

But I didn't want to think about any of that while Kane's hands explored
my body, touching me, exciting me. I had to stifle a moan when he cupped my
breast and squeezed it gently. His other hand slid down my back, cupped my
ass, and pulled me tight against him. I felt the evidence of his arousal against my
stomach. It excited me in a way I'd only imagined possible.

Kane nipped at my lower lip, drawing a groan from me. He eased his hand
under my shirt and pulled down my bra. He twisted the nipple between his
thumb and forefinger, pinching it and causing it to harden immediately.

"Do you want me to stop, little elf?" he asked.

"No," I gasped. I threw my head back, giving Kane the green light to slide his
lips down my throat and over my pulse point. He sucked the spot right beneath
my ear, pulling the blood to the surface and marking me.

"Touch me, Mari," he whispered, his breath hot against my neck.

I tangled my fingers in his thick black hair and held him to my neck. With my other hand, I caressed the front of his red velvet pants. Kane let loose a gasping breath as my fingers brushed his hard shaft and slid down the length. I stroked him until he trembled under my touch.

Kane took a step back, drawing a protesting whine and glare from me, but he just smiled as he dropped to his knees. He smirked, a cocky, I'm-about-to-be-bad look crossing his face. He pushed my skirt up, leaned forward, and placed an almost chaste kiss on my inner thigh. He slid his nose up my leg until he reached the apex of my thighs. He mouthed at my still clothed warm center, sending a tremble through me. I sucked in a deep breath and held it.

Kane twisted his fingers in my underwear, looked up at me, and as soon as I nodded, he yanked, tearing the worn underwear along the frayed seam. They disintegrated and for a second, I thought maybe Kane had done it by sheer willpower. He let them fall to the floor as he leaned close and slowly licked the lips of my pussy.

My head fell back against the wall, and I had to bite my lip to keep myself from making any noise. When his tongue pushed inside of me, I almost screamed. I tried to push him away, not sure I could keep quiet with his head between my legs. Not that I wanted him to stop. This was all my dreams come true. It was like a Penthouse forum story or something on one of those websites you had to be eighteen to view. It certainly wasn't my life. It couldn't be. I didn't do stuff like this. Men didn't do stuff like this to me.

But Kane was right there, his head between my legs, his fingers wrapped around my wrists, holding them at my sides. I squeezed my eyes shut and concentrated on not moaning in ecstasy.

Kissing Kane was a dream come true, but holy shit, the things the man did with his mouth were amazing. I was a complete puddle of need when he finally pulled away, leaving me throbbing and aching with desire.

He rose to his feet, his hands on my ass, his body flush against mine, his erection digging into my stomach. I pushed a hand past the waistband of his pants—no underwear, I should have known—took his cock in my hand and stroked it roughly. He moaned in my ear, a sinful sound that made my blood boil.

I dropped to my knees and pushed him back a couple of steps, desperate to give him as good as he'd given me. Kane moaned again, the filthy sound filling my head. I yanked his pants down just enough to take him in my mouth, my thumb and forefinger wrapped around the base of his cock, my tongue swirling around the tip.

Kane's fingers tangled in my hair, pulling me close, his cock sliding deep into my mouth, bumping the back of my throat. He rocked back and forth, grunting quietly as he fucked my mouth.

I glanced up at him, his head thrown back, eyes closed, his chest heaving as he sucked in a deep breath. God, he was fucking perfect. And I was the one bringing those sounds out of him.

Kane must have seen me looking up at him because he took my arm and dragged me to my feet. His lips crashed into mine, the kiss consuming me. We stood wrapped in each other's arms, chests heaving, bodies throbbing with need.

Kane chuckled. "This is not what I expected to happen when I left for work today. Or when I asked you to go out tonight."

I laughed and pressed my face against his shoulder. "Well, I've been hoping this would happen for weeks." I peeked at him out of the corner of my eye. "I can't believe I just told you that."

"I can't believe you didn't tell me sooner." He lifted me and carried me the ten steps to Santa's sleigh. He climbed inside and sat down, me on his lap, my knees on either side of his thighs. I put my hands on the back of the sleigh, on either side of his head.

Kane rested his hands on my hips and brushed his nose against mine. "Have you been a naughty elf or a nice elf this Christmas, Mari?"

A wave of desire washed over me, so strong I had to close my eyes for a minute. I exhaled.

"I've been naughty, Santa," I whispered.

Kane's sharp intake of breath and his cock hardening between my legs told me he approved of this game.

"Try to be a good little elf and keep your hands right there," he said. "Don't move until I tell you to."

Holy shit.

I liked it when he was bossy and told me what to do. It sent an arousing tingle shooting through me.

"What are you thinking, Mari?" he asked.

I blushed and shook my head. I couldn't tell him.

Or could I?

I glanced down at my elf costume, my mind racing in a million different directions. I'd come this far; I might as well go all the way. He was obviously into the game. I wondered how far I could push him. I leaned forward and put my lips to his ear.

"I want you to unwrap me and play with me like I'm your favorite Christmas present. I want to be naughty, Santa. Can you help me be naughty?"

Kane growled, the sound rumbling deep in his chest. He leaned forward, caught my bottom lip between his teeth, and sucked gently. He ran his hands up and down my sides, then he pushed them beneath my shirt and tugged it over my head. He dropped it on the floor, followed by my bra.

I gasped as the cold air hit me, bringing goosebumps to the surface of my skin. Kane's hands were warm against my skin. He squeezed my breast, plucking and twisting the nipple with his fingers. He kissed my neck, his lips sliding up my jaw to my ear. He nipped at the lobe.

"I need you to be a very quiet elf," he whispered. "You cannot make a sound. Do you understand me?"

I nodded.

He squeezed my breast. "Yes, Santa," he ordered.

"Y-yes Santa," I stammered.

Kane moved his hand down my stomach, his fingers dancing over my pussy. I whimpered as his fingers slowly explored me, his sinfully full lips kissing a hot, wet trail down my neck and across my shoulders.

"Are you wet for me, little elf?" he asked. His finger slipped between the lips of my pussy, and he smiled against my neck. "Mm, you are. I can feel how much you want me." A second finger joined the first, caressing me, his thumb brushing against my clit, making it pulse with need as he teased me.

I whimpered, the immense room swallowing the sound. Kane stopped, his hand still between my legs, not moving. But it was there, and I knew if he wanted to, he could make me cum in a matter of seconds with just those two fingers and his thumb.

His eyes were dark and hooded, the pupils blown wide with lust. He wrapped his fingers in my hair and held my head in place, forcing me to look at him.

"Remember what I said. Quiet, little elf."

"Y...y...yes, Santa." A breathy gasp left me when he moved his fingers the tiniest bit. Heat blasted through me. I wanted to move, wanted to grind myself against his hand until those long, thick fingers were inside me, fucking me.

Kane released my hair and slid his arm around my waist. He tugged me close. "Do it," he ordered.

I didn't have to be told twice. My hips shot forward, seeking the friction I so desperately wanted. Kane's hand and fingers were huge. He easily cupped me, the palm of his hand pressed against my clit, his fingers splitting me open, but not quite inside me. I gasped, but somehow held back the moans of pleasure threatening to burst out of me. I rutted against him, gyrating in his lap, my knuckles white as I gripped the back of the seat.

"Do you like that, little elf? Do you want me inside of you, my fingers inside of you, opening you up so you can take my cock?"

"Yes, please."

Two of Kane's fingers slammed into me, scissoring me open. He buried his fingers deep inside of me, pulling them forward, hitting my sweet spot. I buried my face against the side of Kane's neck and moaned obscenely.

He did it again and again until I came undone, my walls clenching his fingers as I came, his name a curse on my lips. Kane pushed his pants down and pulled his cock free. He stroked it roughly as he continued fucking me with his fingers.

"Condom," he grunted. "Tucked in the belt."

I found the condom tucked behind the black leather belt, ripped the foil packet open, and slid it down Kane's length. Once it was in place, he lifted me, holding me over his substantial length. He lowered me onto his throbbing cock, his eyes rolling back in his head when he was fully seated.

He buried himself inside me, his enormous cock filling me completely. As I watched, he put his fingers in his mouth and sucked, a pleased groan rumbling through his chest. "Damn, you taste good. So good." He kissed me, the tang of me still on his lips. "Hold on, sweetheart."

I wrapped my hands around the back of his neck and Kane grabbed my ass with both hands, yanking me forward, thrusting into me at the same time. I dug my fingers into his shoulders, holding on tightly as he pulled my hips down to meet his, pumping wildly into me. I rode him hard, my breasts bouncing in his face as he urged me on, enticing me to move faster, to ride him harder, to *fuck* him harder.

Kane buried his face between my breasts, biting, licking, and sucking every part of my skin he could reach. His hands were tight on my ass, his cock so deep inside me that his pelvic bone pressed against my clit. It didn't take long before I came unglued, plunging over the edge, the orgasm pulsating through me, the slick of my juices covering Kane as I came.

He was insatiable, slamming into me repeatedly, his feet braced against the floor as his hips snapped up to meet mine. The sleigh slid several inches across its raised platform from the force of his movements. Despite my exhaustion, I felt another orgasm building, right on the heels of the first, a high keening noise escaping me as Kane fucked me into oblivion.

His hips flexed several times, and then he came with a satisfied grunt. He loosened the tight grip he had on my ass, his hands coming up to tangle in my hair. He kissed me, growling deep in his throat as our tongues met.

"That was amazing, little elf."

"Mm, thank *you*, Santa." I took his head in my hands, my forehead pressed to his, kissing him until I couldn't breathe. "That was unexpected, but fun. Who knew Santa was so good at sex?"

Kane threw his head back and laughed. "Who knew elves were so naughty?"

It was my turn to laugh. "Who knew Santa was so naughty?"

Suddenly serious, he ducked his head to look into my eyes. "Are you okay? Are we okay?"

"We're fabulous, Kane. Don't worry."

He rubbed his hands up and down my legs, over the boots and under my skirt. "I love this outfit. You look so damn sexy in it, it's hard to keep my hands off you."

A door slammed on the other side of the building. I heard footfalls echoing off the concrete walls. I quickly climbed off Kane's lap and did my best to straighten my clothes. He shot to his feet and dragged his pants up. Without a word, we separated, me heading for the far side of the display while Kane worked on setting Santa's sleigh straight. When Clyde came around the corner, we looked like we were busily cleaning the display.

"I thought I heard something up here," he said. He leaned against the red and white striped pillar. He looked out of place in his security guard uniform in the middle of Toy Land. "Scared me for a minute."

"It's just us," I replied. "Cleaning up. No trouble here." Out of the corner of my eye, I saw Kane smirk.

Clyde laughed. "Of course not. What kind of mischief would Santa and his elf get into, anyway?" He winked. "You two should go home. It's late."

I giggled. I couldn't help it. It burst out of me, unhindered. Clyde gave me a funny look before he turned on his heel and walked away.

"Go home, Mari!" he yelled.

Kane grabbed me from behind, pushed the hair off my neck, and kissed me. "You ready to go?

I nodded. "Yeah. Let's stop and get a drink. Something warm and sweet."

"Like you," he whispered. "Warm and sweet."

A tingle raced through me, and I shivered. Kane laughed, took my hand, and led me out of Santa's Toy Land.

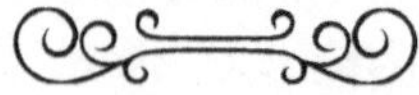

One Year Later

Kane held my hand as we made our way through Fielding's. In his other hand were the bags of Christmas gifts we'd bought. Along with a few other things.

We stopped in front of Santa's display and watched this year's Santa and his elf as they wrangled a group of children and took several pictures. The elf looked frazzled and out of sorts. I wondered if I had looked like that when I'd been Santa's elf.

Kane rested his hand on my barely there baby bump. "Next year we can bring our little one to get their picture taken. I can wear my Santa suit and you can wear your elf costume. What do you think, little elf?"

I blushed and shook my head. "I think maybe we should get new costumes for a family photo. Ours have been a little ... naughty. We need something a little nicer."

Kane threw his head back and laughed. "Okay, love. You're right. New costumes for both of us. And for our baby elf." He kissed the top of my head. "You ready to go home?"

I nodded. "Yeah. I'd like to see if I can still fit in the costume."

A smile spread across Kane's face. "I love that idea." He pressed a kiss to my cheek. "And I love you, little elf."

"I love you, Santa."

We ignored the weird looks we got from the couple standing near us as we hurried from the store into our own winter wonderland.

Kissing in the Closet

Shae Coon

1

JAMES

Bright multicolored strobe lights bounced around the crowded club while fog spilled around our legs, clouding the thick humid air. My best friend and partner Kyle Vanderholt swayed liquidly with a heavy techno beat beside me as club-goers drunkenly grinded against each other to the traditional Christmas song. Violet Delights in downtown Dallas is the place to be if you're anyone who's anyone in the gay community. And Kyle Vanderholt is that anyone.

After coming out to his wealthy and very conservative family, they—in stereotypical form—shunned him. Still, by then, Kyle had already made a name for himself in the community, dressing some of the most recognizable up-and-coming artists and performers. And when the Lucas Torrid, abstract artist extraordinaire, discovered his work, word spread like wildfire. Tonight, we were celebrating our first seven-digit order for Kyle's clothes, bags, and jewelry, which were soon to be premiered at a boutique Lucas's wife owned in New York.

Where do I fit in? I was the guy with the impressive portfolio that consisted of investments into some small businesses ranging from app developers all the way to big-name real estate developers. So, when Kyle came to me a year ago and asked for some start-up cash, I jumped at the opportunity to help my childhood friend. Now, I was an equal partner at Holt & Kade designs. I argued against my name being on the label, but he told me to, and I quote, "Shut my bitch-ass up," so I never brought it up again. That's just how Kyle was, and I loved the guy.

Don't get me wrong—I swung my bat for the ladies, and while Kyle was in his prime and happy finding new man candy—his words not mine—every few nights, I was looking for *the one*. What? You thought I was the typical hot playboy? Well, at 6'3" with dark brown hair, icy-blue eyes, and a body that I worked and trained like an MMA fighter, I suppose the hot part is correct.

The problem was that all women wanted—well, all of that, my wallet, and a night in heaven with me buried deep inside them. And that was fine back in my early twenties, but now tipping the edge of thirty, I wanted something real. I wanted a woman that saw me. Not my connections, money, or just a pretty face and a rocking time in the bedroom. I wanted someone who could hold an intelligent conversation, but alas, my perfect woman had so far alluded me.

"I hope you don't mind, but I met this *senorita* at an art opening and invited her out to help us party," Kyle yelled over the music.

"Brother, invite all of Oaklawn! This is your night," I shouted back and slapped him on the back.

"Our night, motherfucker! Don't pull that humble B.S. with me. I would be sitting in my shithole apartment crying tears into polyester right now if it weren't for you." He waved my words away with a flourish of his hand.

"Okay, Okay," I held my hands up in surrender, "our night." I laughed, but then that amusement turned to pure primal lust when my eyes landed on a gorgeous brunette being dragged through the crowd by her blonde friend.

My dick strained against my zipper as she got closer, and my eyes roamed her body: long tanned legs, wide hips made for my hands, pert tits stuffed in the tight bodice of her dress, and a long swan-like neck that my lips would love to explore. Her lips were plush, and her smile could outshine the sun. A heart-shaped face and eyes as brown as the darkest chocolate. Fuck, she was perfection.

She stumbled in her heels and laughed as her friend tugged her along. *Or are they lovers? Shit, I hope not.* My eyes stayed riveted on her as they came closer, and Kyle jumped to hug the blonde. My heart thumped heavily against my chest when I realized the blonde must be the girl Kyle met at the art opening. When he gestured to me, I gave a small wave.

He addressed the brunette next, then hugged her too, and for the first time in my life, I was jealous of my friend. Kyle turned to me and gestured to the blonde. "This is Lacey," he shouted. I nodded and shook Lacey's hand, and I didn't miss the lustful look she gave me. "And this is her friend, Allana." Allana.

A beautiful name for a beautiful woman. I shook Allana's hand, but unlike her friend, I was not as quick to let her go.

"Allana," I said and gave her a dimpled smile.

Her cheeks blushed, and she chuckled. "Uh-oh, I can tell you're trouble," she teased, and her pure, light spirit and melodic laughter warmed my chest.

I leaned into her. "You have no idea, beautiful," I said and made sure my lips grazed the shell of her ear. She beamed up at me, and my dick became painfully desperate for relief. Relief only Allana could provide.

The next hour was spent laughing at the shit Kyle and I got into as kids and talking about Kyle's creations. When he went on about how I helped him and how I was the greatest man he knew, I would steal glances at Allana to gauge her reaction. I expected to see dollar signs in those brown depths, that hunger to use me and not in just the carnal way, but every time I caught her eye, she would peer up at me with ... admiration. There was no hidden motive, no selfish gold-digging plots. Nothing but awe and attraction, though she tried to hide the latter.

This woman had me snagged on her hook, and I was ready to take it to the next level. However, just as I was about to make a move, her words put a halt to my plans. "So why aren't you out there," she pointed to the dance floor, "finding some man-candy to woo?" At first, her question confused me, then like a gong, it vibrated through my head.

She thinks I'm gay.

That's why she seems so comfortable with me. Maybe even why she isn't trying to get anything from me. After all, if I'm gay, she can't use her feminine wiles to get what she wants. Fuck! Just when I think I found the perfect girl she may just be like all the rest. But damn, she's cool as shit, and I've enjoyed talking and laughing with her. It's only been an hour, and I already feel like I have a deep connection with her. Do I want to give that up? Do I confess I'm straight and see if she suddenly turns and possibly lose what we have? Or do I play along and keep what we do have—even if it could only ever be friendship?

I can't lose this girl. Mind made up, I looked out at the dancing bodies and laughed at Kyle dry humping Lacey, throwing her into a fit of giggles. I turned back to Allana with a smirk. "I'm not that type of guy." I shrugged and took a swig of my beer.

"And what type of guy are you?" she asked and sipped on her whiskey. *Damn, the girl can even hit the hard shit.* I watched her swallow the burning liquid with not so much as a wince, and the image of her taking me deep in her throat as I blew a load of my cum down that slender throat had me subtly adjusting myself under the tabletop.

"I've done the hit it and quit it thing. Now I want the real thing. Connection, passion. Love." I stared into her brown orbs, pleading for this to be the real her.

She gave me a model-worthy smile. "That is one of the sweetest things I have ever heard from a man's lips. It's just too bad…" She trailed off, and her eyes saddened, and I wanted to tell her to finish, but Kyle and Lacey picked that time to stumble drunkenly over and demand more shots.

"No more for you, Miss Lacey." Allana laughed and tapped her friend's nose. Shit, she's leaving. "I think it's time to get you home."

"We're going to head out too," I concurred, and both Allana and I got a round of boos from our drunk friends.

"But I didn't get any D," Kyle whined.

"Me either," Lacey followed, and Allana laughed hysterically.

"It's a gay bar, Lacey. These dicks aren't for you." Allana shook her head, still chuckling.

"Why not? Oh right, you found the only straight dude here." She waggled a finger at me, and I stilled. *Shit, was I just caught in my own web of lies?*

"He's not straight, Lacey. You just want D so bad you're looking in all the wrong places." Allana rolled her eyes, and I was both relieved and disheartened by her words.

"Right." Lacey gave my body a drunken perusal before tapping my cheek sloppily. "Sure he is," she said, then attempted to wink at me. "Okay then. If there's no dick to be had, I'm out!" She started to walk away, and with a quick wave, Allana followed but not before I reached out and grabbed her small hand. Immediately, fireworks exploded under my skin when we touched, my chest tightened, and the urge to press my lips to her pouty ones became overwhelming.

Wrangling in my need, I brought her back to me, making sure to keep our bodies separate. "Give me your number," I said, then unlocked my phone and handed it to her. Taking it, she called her own cell, then handed me back mine. With one last smile, she kissed my cheek and walked away, leaving behind a hunger I'd never felt before.

Allana was mine now. Just not in the way I craved.

2

6 months later

Allana

"So, how was Barbados?" Lacey asked around a mouth full of sandwich.

Once a week, we had lunch together at the same cafe down the road from the construction company I worked for. The little café was decked out in red, green, and silver garland. Multi-colored twinkling lights lined each window, and a large wreath hung from the door, welcoming customers to come and enjoy their delicious holiday treats.

Though, ever since Lacey started working for Kyle Vanderholt as his PA, our lunches have backed off to whenever she had the time. I wasn't upset, though. After all, James and I were practically joined at the hip and had been since we met at the club six months ago. He had become my best guy friend, and I adored him.

Yeah, he was mega hot and rich, but that wasn't what made him great. Don't get me wrong, his looks were a big plus, but they could also be a big negative when you couldn't stop staring at your best friend's abs while sunbathing on the beach of a tropical paradise. Especially when he caught you and gave you that panty-melting smirk of his.

But I digress. What made James great was … just being James. He was intelligent, funny, inspirational, and the most caring man I had ever met. He was genuine in everything he said and did, and I found myself in awe of the man.

"You would know. You and Kyle have gone like what? Ten times?" I teased.

"Yeah, but I'm not talking about my very gay friend and me. I'm talking about you and your very questionably gay friend." She threw back, and I groaned at the fact that we're having this conversation again.

"Lacey, James. Is. Gay." I shook my head in agitation, the bell on my reindeer antlers jingling merrily. "How many times do we have to have this argument?"

"I. Don't. Buy. It. And we will continue to have this argument until the day you open your eyes," she said and took a huge bite of her sandwich.

I sighed. "Just drop it. Barbados was beautiful, and we had a lot of fun. Although I am happy to be home. I love Christmas in Texas." I beamed because Christmas was my absolute favorite holiday, and Christmas in Texas? You couldn't find a more festive place during the holiday. However, my holiday cheer was plagued with one concern...

"Do you think I look like a gold digger? Or someone just looking to get something from James?"

Lacey stared at me like I just told her the red and green Leopardo fabric she spent weeks acquiring for Kyle's holiday collection was no longer in style. "Are you shitting me? What kind of stupid question is that? He offers all these trips, nights out, and gifts. I believe you turn his ass down every time, only for him to insist until he's worn you down. So no, you do not look like an opportunistic hoe," she defended.

"Not exactly what I said, but okay. I just don't want James to ever think I'm friends with him for anything but for who he is." I shrugged and picked at the bread of my turkey sub.

Lacey's hand squeezed mine across the table, and the look she gave me has the back of my eyes stinging. "He loves you, Lana, and it just so happens that's how he shows it. So, keep doing what you're doing and being who you are."

"You're right. I'm being silly. James has always been honest with me. He would tell me if he felt I was being a mooch."

"Right! Now let's get one of those big ass snowman cookies to share," she proclaimed and nearly sprinted to the bakery counter.

Walking down Main Street in Grapevine, I watched as women and men dressed in their business suits scurried along the crosswalks to wait an hour in line for their favorite lunch spot. The weather was a chilly fifty degrees—an actual low temperature for Texas in December—and the smell of even colder weather to come had my hopes of a white Christmas lifting.

My phone vibrated in the hidden pocket of my sweater dress that I bought on sale for twelve bucks. Plucking the outdated device from my pocket, my lips stretched into a wide grin when I saw his smiling face on the screen.

"Hello, handsome. Calling to make sure I didn't run off with the cabana boy after all?" I teased. During our time in Barbados, James insisted that the waiter was purposely making sure he got our cabana when we hit the beach every afternoon to, in his words, "Check out his girl." I simply laughed it off, but I could have sworn James was jealous. I knew I had to be wrong and that it was just him being protective. Still, a part of me got a thrill from the thought that he didn't want another man to even wait on me.

"Not funny, Lana. The guy was a douche at best and a total dick at worst." He returned, irritation clear in his tone.

"Okay, okay. So, what's up?" I made it to my car and docked my phone to let the Bluetooth take over, then cranked up the heat. James' deep, sexy timbre came through my speakers, and goosebumps rose along my skin. James had always been my weakness. If the guy wasn't gay, I would be begging for a piece of him. Pathetic? Maybe, but I stand by it.

"Are you with Lacey?" he asked gruffly.

"We just finished up lunch. I'm heading back to the office. Why?"

Lacey and James' relationship was … tolerable. As in, they barely tolerated each other. I wasn't sure why they clashed so much, but the two mixed like oil and water.

"I just got a call from Philipe," he growled, and I winced at yet another attempt by Lacey to set James up with another client of Kyle's. "She gave him my damn number, Lana. I'm going to strangle her with the new line of cashmere scarves Kyle's been pimping if she doesn't stop this shit."

"I know. I'm sorry. I'll talk—"

"No! I can fight my own battles. The only reason I called you was to get her on the phone, seeing as she won't answer my calls." He sighed in frustration, and I felt for my friend. Lacey was a notorious matchmaker. However, she was horrible at it! Sometimes I thought she picked the worst matches for James and me on purpose.

"I'm sorry. If it helps, she set me up with some guy she met at a bar in Cowtown. I guess since she's the one that met him at a bar and not me, it doesn't go against my no bar-booty rule." I rolled my eyes.

There's silence on the other side of the line before James cleared his throat and asked, "When's the date?"

"Tomorrow. He's picking me up at seven," I huffed.

"Okay. Same as always?" he asked, referring to the deal we have for our dates. Nights we go out on dates we get ready at the other's place then return after to dish out the details.

"You know it," I chirped, sounding happier than I actually am about the upcoming date.

"Sounds good," he said, a hint of sadness coating his voice.

"Everything okay?" I pulled up to my building but didn't get out. My sales guys would have to wait.

"Yeah. I gotta get back to work. Talk to you later, babe."

"Wait! Are we still doing Christmas at my place?" I asked. It wasn't just James and me that had become good friends. Our parents hit it off too and were taking a Christmas cruise together, of all things, so it was just James and me this year.

"I'll be there with jingle bells on."

I laughed at his cheesy pun. "Okay, you nut. See you tomorrow." We disconnected, but I couldn't stop feeling that something was going on with my friend. In the last few months, he'd seemed a bit ... off. One moment we would be laughing and teasing each other as we decorated the tree or baked cookies that ended up being inedible, only to turn melancholy the next moment. Then there were the times that I swore I saw heat in his stare as he helped me pick a cocktail dress for a work function or when I would talk about anything remotely sexual. But that was ridiculous and probably just my undersexed and natural attraction to the model-sexy friend I loved.

Either way, the deep longing for him to be straight needed to stay hidden in the dark pit of "never gonna happen" land in my mind. But hey, a girl can dream, right?

3

JAMES

I was going to kill Lacey Cambell. Not because she gave some random guy my number—well, not just because she gave some random guy my number. I was tired of meeting the guys she set me up with and playing the dickhead in the hope that they would never want to speak to me again. It sucked having to be the bad guy, but I only had myself to blame for being too chicken-shit to confess the truth to my best friend and dream girl.

But all the shitty set-ups didn't compare to the dread of watching Allana dress up and leave with another man like I would do once again tonight. I loved every moment we spent together, but my growing possessiveness almost got the best of me when I would see the fucker at the door with some cheesy bouquet of flowers or a bottle of wine. Lana, being as sweet as she was, would take the offering with grace and a smile even though she hated wine and didn't like the thought of flowers being plucked and used for such purposes only to die days later.

She was the best person I knew, and it was getting increasingly harder to keep her in the friend zone. I had a decision to make. I either nutted up and told her the truth or kept going on with this charade and be miserable the rest of my life. The answer would seem obvious, but it no longer seemed so simple when that answer could also bring down what we currently had.

As I walked to my car, the steadily dropping temperature that threatened snow matched my chilly mood. Another night of watching my girl get ready for another man. Fan-fucking-tastic.

The next evening at six sharp, Lana knocked once then entered my house. "Honey, I'm home," she sang and found me in my room getting ready for a night of binge-watching Netflix movies while I waited up for her.

She stepped into my room, but her steps faltered, and her eyes widened when she found me bare chested, the pajama pants with Christmas wreaths all over them she gifted me with last week hung low on my hips, skin still damp from my shower. I may have been putting on a show, and by the heat that flared in her eyes the color of hot cocoa, I was doing a damn good job. Except for the little—well maybe not little—fact that the look on her face had me wanting to tear off her clothes like a gift on Christmas morning. *Really James? Christmas themed sex puns?*

Leaning against the dresser to hide my growing problem, I gestured to the bathroom. "It's all yours." When she didn't speak, I stood and moved toward her. Leaning into her space, I inhaled the gingerbread body spray I bought her before bringing my lips to her ear. "Lana," I whispered, and the small gasp she let out had my nerves lighting up like the Rockefeller Center Christmas tree, but before I could make a move, she stepped back and shook her head.

"Sorry, I was lost in thought there." She laughed.

"Oh, yeah?" I smirked. "What were you thinking about?" I asked, knowing damn well where her thoughts were.

"Oh, uh, just about tonight. Maybe this one will actually work out. Wouldn't that be a Christmas miracle?" She giggled, and even though I knew she was lying, the thought of her falling for this guy didn't sit right with me. Crossing my arms over my chest, I nodded. "Yeah, maybe. I'll let you get ready," I said and headed for the door.

"You're not going to talk to me while I get ready?" she asked in disappointment.

On date nights, I would sit outside the bathroom, and we would talk about different shit and joke around about all the things that could go wrong, but tonight I couldn't bring myself to do it.

"I can't tonight, babe. I have some work I didn't finish at the office, and with the break coming up, I need to get it done," I lied and felt like a piece of shit for it. Especially when her eyes turned sad and her lips tipped down.

But she quickly schooled herself and smiled that radiant smile of hers. "Okay, Mister Big Shot, go do your thing. I'll be done quick, then we can talk before I head out."

"Sounds good," I said, then headed to my office to try and do some actual work.

As I booted up my laptop, the thought of Lana in my shower naked and drenched had my dick rock hard, and my frustration ramped up to one hundred. If I didn't get a hold of myself, I was going to be sporting an impressive hard-on when it was time for her to leave.

Deciding to take matters into my own hands—literally—I shut and locked my office door and sat in the leather armchair opposite my desk. Lifting my ass just enough to pull my pants beneath my ass, my dick sprang free, and pre-cum was already wetting the tip. Using it as a lubricant, I began to stroke myself. I started off with long slow strokes and thoughts of Lana's wet tits clouding my vision.

"Fuck, yes," I moaned and tightened my grip, imagining it's Lana's tight pussy as she rode me, her lithe body blushing with exertion as she went buck wild on my dick. My strokes began to speed up, and my hips thrust into my hand as the vision of Lana throwing her head back in ecstasy, calling out my name as she came on my dick. "Yes, cum for me, Lana. Uuuh, fuuuck!" I groaned as my balls drew up and my cum spilled onto my stomach and hand. My breaths were labored, and my heart was beating a mile a minute as I slowly stroked myself to completion. However, when the high of orgasm faded, the need for Lana didn't. "Fuck." Standing, I cleaned myself up with the tissues on the side table and got back to work.

Forty-five minutes later, there was a timid knock on my office door, and then Lana stepped inside. Her hair was up in a tight ponytail hanging to just below her shoulders, a red poinsettia barrette nestled on the side of her head. Her makeup was minimal aside from her bright red lips. She was dressed casually in black skinny jeans, ankle boots, and a deep red cotton peasant top. She was my every dream come true. She was intelligent, hilarious, gorgeous, and had the biggest heart. Every time I thought I couldn't fall for her anymore, each time, I was proven wrong.

She stood before me, hands out to her side, a shy smile on her face. "Well, how do I look?"

Leaning back in my chair, I scanned her from head to toe, not bothering to hide the carnal need that I was sure burned in my stare. Once I finished my perusal of her delicious curves, I beckoned her to me with a crook of my finger.

As she swallowed deep, I could see her nipples harden beneath her top, and I had to adjust myself beneath my desk.

Slowly she made her way to me, and when she reached my desk, I stood, grabbed her hips, and lifted her to sit on the edge. Wedging myself between her legs, I could feel the heat of her pussy against my pajama-covered cock. She looked up at me with large doll eyes, flames of desire battling to break free. She wanted me, but my lie was keeping her at bay. "James," she whispered, and with my name floating on her beautiful lips, my decision was made.

"Lana, I need to tell—" *Ding dong.* The doorbell interrupted my confession, and when I saw the shutters come down in her eyes, I knew my moment was gone.

With a chuckle, she pushed at my chest and stood. "He's early. Guess that's a checkmark for the so-far-so-good section," she said and began to fidget with her top, then tightened her already perfect ponytail—her only tell that I'd thrown her off balance. "Shall we?" she asked, and I gave her my best, fake I'm-not-dying-inside smile.

"Sure." I gestured for her to precede me.

When we made it to the living room, she grabbed her purse and phone then turned to me for help putting on her jacket. When she turned back to me, concern swam in her eyes. "You'll be here when I get back?" she asked.

Running my fingers over her ponytail, I nodded. "Of course," I reassured. "Where else would I be?"

"Nowhere. I just... Nevermind. I think I'm just nervous. I hate first dates." She laughed humorlessly.

"Then don't go," I said too eagerly, and when I thought she was about to agree, the damn bell rang again.

"I have to go." She gave me a peck on the cheek, then turned and opened the door to greet the man waiting for her—waiting for my girl—and then she was gone.

⁂

It was half-past ten when the second *Die Hard* movie ended, and I brought up the next one when I heard a car pull up, doors slamming, then Lana's elevated voice.

"Go find some other girl to play with, you jerk. Not every woman is desperate to get beneath you," she yelled.

"Whatever you say, you frigid bitch!" a male voice yelled back, and I immediately saw red. Strike that. What I saw was me murdering the bastard.

I sprinted for the door, ready to carve the guy like a Christmas ham when the door swung open and a disheveled Lana marched in. She slammed the door, ripped the poinsettia clip from her hair, and threw her purse to the ground, not caring that the contents slid across the floor. "Errrr, why do men have to be so disgusting!" she growled to no one in particular. Then, as though she remembered where she was, she turned to me, eyes wild and sprouts of hair coming loose from her ponytail. "And then they have the balls to try and make us feel like it's our fault!" She slapped her thighs in disbelief, and while my temper was still simmering, I couldn't help but adore the "crazy woman" vibe she had going on. "Don't you laugh at me, James Kade," she scolded and poked a finger in my chest.

Chuckling, I grabbed her wrist and kissed the tip of her finger, and when she bit her bottom lip at the intimate touch, my anger melted away only to be replaced with a lustful yearning. "Calm down there, tiger. I wasn't laughing at you. You're just too damn adorable when you're on a tirade." I brushed a piece of chestnut hair from her face. "You're beautiful. Even when you're ready to tear a man's balls off."

With a roll of her eyes and a scoff, she walked away, leaving me to watch her pert ass in her tight jeans. "Okay, okay, I'm sorry. You want me to go after the guy? I have no problem kicking his ass. Especially after what I just heard him call you." My temper started to rise up again when she winced at the reminder of what that prick called her.

"You heard that?" she asked, and the shame that coated her tone has me reaching for my keys and heading for the door. "Where are you going?"

She grabbed my bicep, and I turned steely eyes on her. "What's the fucker's name?"

"Why? What are you going to do? Go around the entire city just asking random people if they've seen him?" she smarted off.

"Of course not. If the guy is like any other, then he's headed to the nearest club to pick up a willing piece of ass." Again, she winced at my words. Dropping my head back on my shoulders, I silently prayed to the ceiling gods to give me strength. I knew I needed to take a step back and stop trying to fix the problem and just listen. "Fine. I won't go looking for the asshole." I dropped my keys on the side table. "Come on, tell me what happened." I guided her to the couch, where she plopped down with a heavy sigh and stared at the Christmas tree lit up in the corner, the slightest smile tipping her lips.

"I'm not sure, really. We were actually having a decent time. He was funny, smart, good-looking..." I made a keep-it-moving gesture with my hand. I didn't need to hear that shit. "Then when he walked me to his car after dinner, it's like a switch flipped. He backed me against the car and started kissing me. When I pushed him away, he said, and I quote, 'come on baby, you know you want me.' Who the hell actually says that?!" she exclaimed and threw her hands up.

"Damn. He really said that?" I huffed out a laugh.

"Yes! I pushed him off and said I wasn't down for that and demanded he take me home. The ride back was pretty quiet until he started mumbling about how he couldn't believe he wasted his time on someone who couldn't even kiss. That kissing me was like kissing a frozen fish. Of course, I made a crack about him practicing on frozen fish, which pissed him off more. And well, the rest you heard." She finished, and I had to stop myself from punching a hole in the nearest wall.

Lana was everything a woman should be, but her self-esteem was shit even though she was drop-dead, pin-up sexy. "You really think I'm frigid?" she asked in a low murmur, and my heart squeezed at the vulnerability in her tone. She looked up at me, her eyes glassy with tears she would never let fall. Not for an asshole like him. "Do you think I kiss like a frozen fish?" She rubbed at her nose to stop the tingling of unshed tears.

Pulling the hair tie from her hair, I never took my eyes from hers when I answered, "No, Lana, I don't. You are one of the most passionate women I have ever known. You take on anything and everything with enthusiasm and heart, so there's no way you could be frigid," I assert, but I can still see the uncertainty in her eyes. "Come on. You can stay with me tonight. I'll sleep on the couch, and in the morning, we can talk more about it, or we can just eat our weight in pancakes. Deal?"

Her smile lit up my entire being, and the need to kiss her became overwhelming, but she was too vulnerable right then. So rather than taking her in my arms and ravaging her, I stood and helped her up and headed to my room.

Entering my walk-in closet, I pulled out a pair of my boxers and a T-shirt for her to sleep in. "But what if I am a bad kisser," Lana asked from behind me.

I turned and saw gone was the vulnerable little girl from moments ago, and in her place was the curious little kitten I've always known her to be. Handing her the clothes, I smiled down at her. "You're not."

"But how do you know for sure?" she asked, determined.

I ran a hand through my shaggy hair in frustration. "I just do, Lana. What do you want me to say?"

She shrugged. "I don't want you to say anything. I want you to kiss me," she said plainly. As though her words didn't just rock my fucking world.

"What? You want...Why?" I stammered, and I wanted to kick my own ass for even thinking to fight her on this, but she had just came from a shitty date, and she was just acting out. *Right?*

She rocked back and forth on her heels. "Because we're friends, and friends help each other out. I can read you like a book, so if I do kiss like crap, I'll be able to tell by your reaction. Granted, I don't have the right parts for you, but it's just a kiss. I don't need to turn you on. I just need to know if the mechanics are on point."

"On point? Jesus, Lana." I fisted my hair with both hands and tried to picture old ladies in their underwear in an effort to call back my growing erection at the thought of finally getting a piece of her.

"You know what I mean." She rolled her eyes. "Pleeeeease, James. One kiss, then I'll drop this it." She pleaded, making prayer hands beneath her chin. When I stood there staring and silent, the hope in her eyes fell away, and she shook her head. "It's okay. It was a stupid idea. Just forget—"

Her words were swallowed up by my lips when they landed hard and brutal on hers, the need to taste her finally breaking free. She hummed against my mouth as the shock faded and her lips loosened against mine, and suddenly everything clicked into place. The part of me that yearned for more—yearned for this woman—became whole.

Our lips moved across each other's effortlessly, as though we'd done this our entire adult life. Like we were meant to kiss each other.

My hands moved into dark strands to tip her head back and run my tongue along the seam of her lips, begging for entry. When her lips parted, I thanked her with a swipe of my tongue against hers. Her moans of pleasure vibrated through my lips and traveled straight to my already straining dick. Guiding her back against the closet island, I grinded my erection against her stomach. She gasped when she feels me against her, and like a woman possessed, she grabbed my ass and thrust her hips forward, desperate for more contact. "Fuck, Lana, you're incredible. I don't know if I can stop." I huffed against her lips.

"Don't. Please, don't stop, James," she pleaded, and when she moved a hand to my cock and squeezed, I was done for.

I knocked her hand away, tore the peasant blouse and bra from her body, and immediately cupped her full ripe breasts. "Pants off, now," I ordered around swipes of my tongue, and felt her kick off her boots before unbuttoning her jeans and dragging them down her legs as far as she could without having to disengage our lips. Wanting her naked, I dropped to a knee and quickly removed the offending material, and with my eyes still locked with hers, I ran my tongue over her lace-covered pussy lips. She threw her head back with a throaty moan then whimpered when my fingers slipped beneath the material and through her drenched folds. "Fuck, baby, is that all for me?" I asked, and she just moaned in response. Dragging her panties down her legs, I kissed and nipped at the silky skin of her thighs. "Answer me."

"Yes, James. It's all for you. Please…"

My fingers came back to her pussy, and I entered one, then two, as I began to suck on her clit. "Please, what? What do you want, Lana?" I asked and added a bite to her clit.

She jumped with a small yelp before sighing and clutching the island behind her. "That! That's so good."

"Mmmm." I hummed against her swollen lips as I feasted on her juices. "Is that all you want, Lana?"

"No, I want…Oh dear God," she groaned. "I want you inside me," she finished, and with one last deep suck of my lips, she orgasmed. Her essence flowed over my tongue as I lapped at her clit, and when she yanked on my hair, I stood and took her lips once more. I let her taste herself on my lips while I dropped my pajama pants and let my dick spring free.

She pulled back, cast her eyes to my cock, and licked her lips like a woman starved, and I was her next meal. Pulling her to me, I growled against her ear. "Another time, baby. Right now, I need to be inside you." I lifted her from her feet and carried her to my bed. Grabbing a condom from the bedside table, I sheathed myself when I heard her giggle. "What?" I cocked an eyebrow.

"Are you wrapping my Christmas present, Mister Kade?" She giggled again, and as I looked at this sexy as fuck woman, lust wasn't the only thing overcrowding my senses, but the boundless love I had for her. *My Lana.*

Climbing onto the bed, I dragged my fingers up her torso and plucked at one tight pink nipple before bringing the sugar plum into my mouth to savor. She moaned and squirmed beneath my mouth, and when both nipples had gotten equal attention, I brought my lips to her ear. "Ready for me to stuff your stocking, baby?" We both still at my words, then burst into laughter.

"Oh my God, you did not just say that!" Lana snickered.

I smiled against her lips. "I did," I chuckled, then deepened the kiss. This time it was a slow, decadent slide of tongue against tongue, lips against lips. Heart against heart. And with the next touch of our tongues, I lined up the head of my cock at her dripping entrance and thrust deep into her tight canal. She bellowed her pleasure against my lips while I cursed against hers.

My body began to tremble with everything I felt for this woman, and when I pulled out to the tip of my cock and dove deep again, her head tipped back, a moan escaping her lips. My lips trailed open, mouthing kisses over her damp skin. At the same time, my hips took on a steady rhythm as if knowing exactly what she needed to feel ultimate pleasure.

When her feet dug into my ass, and the walls of her pussy tightened around me, I knew she was on the edge, so with a swirl of my hips, I grinded against her clit, and she came.

"James!" she cried, the sound of my name on her lips causing my hips to jackhammer forward and my balls to draw tight, and with one final deep plunge, I exploded.

"Yes, Lana. Fuck, yes!" I barked and let the euphoria of the best orgasm of my life take over every cell in my body.

When my climax finally faded, I flipped onto my back and pulled her into my chest. Her hand went to my chest, and her sigh of contentment had me feeling like a king.

I tossed the condom to the floor, and when I felt her breathing become a steady rhythm of sleep, I whispered, "I love you."

4

ALLANA

James moves inside me with hard, strong thrusts, and I can feel the impending orgasm rising from deep inside me. His eyes shine with lust, desire, and love, the latter making my heart speed faster as James makes love to me. "I love you, my Lana," he whispers sweetly in my ear, and when I go to speak the words back, his form fades, and the pull of wakefulness drags me from him.

My eyes fluttered open, and the bright sun shining through the open curtains warmed my skin. I did a full-body stretch with a lazy smile and felt the pull of tight, overused muscles, but my smile slipped when I felt a presence move beside me. Turning my head slowly, I saw my dream guy next to me, eyes latched onto mine, a boyish smile stretching his lips. His eyes were puffy with sleep and the blue twinkle in the sunlight. His hair was an adorable mess atop his head, and my heart thrilled while my brain screamed at me for being such an idiot.

James' smile dropped when I just stared at him, hands clutched in the sheet now pulled to my chin. "Hey, you alright?" he asked and ran his fingers over my forearm. *Oh God, the same fingers that brought me to one of the best orgasms of my life only to be topped by the one brought on by his impressive cock.*

"Uh, I..." My brain scrambled to come up with what to say. "I gotta go," I finally said, then jumped out of bed, taking the sheet with me, which was a terrible idea because now James' perfect body was on display along with his morning erection.

"What? Why?" James asked as I forced my eyes to stop ogling his member and started to gather my clothes.

"I just do. I have stuff to do," I answered dismissively.

"Stuff to do? What the hell, Lana. What's going on?" He stood and put on a pair of pajama bottoms. I fled to the bathroom, where I got dressed and tried to calm myself, but calm never came, so with a counterfeit smile on my lips, I exited the bathroom to find the room empty.

I power walked to the living room where I collected the scattered contents of my purse and made a break for the door, but my escape attempt was thwarted when James stepped in front of it, arms crossed, chiseled torso still on glorious display. "What the fuck is going on, Lana? You're the last one I thought to freak out. Especially when you're the one that begged me to kiss you."

Oh, God, I did, didn't I?

"I know, and I'm so sorry. Is it too late to pretend that all that," I gestured toward the bedroom, "never happened? Just go back to the way it was?" I asked with a hopeful smile.

"Hell yes, it's too late," he sneered, and my hackles rose.

"What? Why?" I repeated his question from earlier.

He hesitated before running a hand through his shaggy hair. "We just can't."

"That's not an answer, James."

He shrugged and dropped his arm. "Take it or leave it," he said, then headed to the kitchen, and I was on his heels.

"Don't walk away from me, James Kade. Why do you even care about last night? You're gay!" I squeaked.

He swung around, with a mix of confusion and rage in his ocean blue eyes. "What?" he asked in disbelief, and I had to admit I was in a bit of disbelief myself. He was gay, yet last night you wouldn't know it. The only thing I could chalk it up to was him just being in the heat of the moment. The friction of body parts, maybe? Either way, he was gay, and it didn't matter how much I wanted him again ... and again and again.

Done with this bizarre conversation, I swung my purse over my shoulder and headed back toward the door. "You know what, James? Keep your reasons. I'm out." I threw up a peace sign as I walked away, head held high.

I heard his heavy footsteps as he same after me. "Lana, stop!" he shouted.

"No, James!" I mocked and swung open the door.

The chilly morning air blasted me in the face, but it was James' next words that had me frozen in place. "Damn it, Lana, I'm not gay!" he proclaimed. "I'm not gay, and I never have been. The night we met, I had given up on finding a woman that saw beyond my looks, money, and influence. Then I met you," he hurried to explain. "You were so beautiful, kind, intelligent, and you seemed to genuinely like me, so when you made the comment about me finding a man to woo, I guess... I guess I figured if you looked at me the way you did because you thought I was gay, then I would take it if it meant keeping you in my life. We had just met, and I was already shit scared to lose you. So, I lied, and I am so sorry, Lana." When he finished, the room was blanketed in silence.

For six months, I'd dreamt of being with this man while chastising myself for wanting him to be something he was not. My heart broke every time he left for a date, then I would feel horrible every time I wished for those dates to go wrong. I cried some nights, believing that I would never find a man like my best friend because the perfect man was not an option. And now he told me exactly what I've wanted to hear. And while most women would most likely feel relief, I felt ... betrayed. Betrayed because with his confession came the glaring fact that the man I thought was my best friend for the last six months, my safe place, the one person I thought I could trust, had been lying to me, therefore making me question our entire friendship.

My heart shattered in an instant, and my eyes clouded with tears. Turning toward the man I loved so profoundly, I stared into his beautiful blue eyes, now filled with anguish, and spoke the words that would end everything we were. "I never want to see you again." Then I walked out the door, and this time, James didn't come after me.

TWO WEEKS LATER
CHRISTMAS EVE

"I still can't believe you were right," I sulked.

After storming out of James' house, I immediately called Lacey, only for her phone to go straight to voicemail. I had forgotten she and Kyle were on a party bender in Milan, and phone service would be spotty on the yacht they chartered. When she did finally get back to me, she confirmed my suspicions and admitted to setting James and me up on crappy dates on purpose, arguing that she wanted James to fess up and for me to remain single until he finally did.

"Hey, I told you I didn't believe the whole gay routine. I just didn't have the proof. What did Kyle say when you asked him why he didn't tell you?" She smiled around a bite of food.

I sighed and slouched back in my chair. "He said because James asked him not to and 'Bros before hoes' and all that crap."

Lacey snorted, and I couldn't help but smile, but my smile dropped when the look of anguish on James' face the last time I saw him flashed across my mind. A part of me understood why he did what he did, but the other part argued that if he truly knew me and cared for me like he claimed to, he would know I didn't want anything from him other than just him. And as the days passed, my heart and brain were in a constant battle. My heart wanted me to run to him and forgive him, but my brain screamed, "Once a liar, always a liar."

"Lana, just forgive the man. I can see you're miserable." I wiped away a rogue tear, and she sighed and grabbed my hand across the table. "Look, I completely understand the hurt you feel, and believe me when I say I tore him a new asshole for it, but also believe me when I say the man is tore up about it."

"How tore up?" I mumbled and gave her a crooked smile.

She laughed and wiggled my hand. "So tore up he would lick your boots if you told him to."

I scrunched up my nose at the thought. "It's been two weeks."

"So?" She shrugged and stuffed another bite of salad in her mouth.

"I've been radio silent with him. I've even ignored the dozens of text messages and gifts he's been sending me."

At that, Lacey's eyes widened. "Please tell me you did not throw out the tickets for the Dallas Stars New Year's Eve game?" she asked in horror.

"No, I haven't, but I should. He can't buy me, Lacey," I admonished.

"Uh, no shit, Sherlock. But I don't think he's trying to buy you."

"How do you figure?" I challenged.

"Because if he was trying to buy you like you're some gold-digging bimbo, he would send you jewelry, lingerie, and shit like that. Instead, he's sending gifts that are personal to you. Hockey tickets, a Kindle Unlimited subscription, passes to ICE at the Gaylord. Do I need to go on?" she asked haughtily.

"No, you do not," I grumbled, then sat straight. "Fine, I will consider calling him. After all, it is Christmas Eve. Happy?"

"Very! And tonight, you and I are hitting the club. We're going to Ho, ho, ho it up, girl!" Lacey beamed and went back to devouring her lunch, and while I couldn't help but laugh at my friend, my thoughts never stopped going over the decision before me. *Sacrifice my heart or my brain?*

5

JAMES

"Helloooo, are you in there?" Kyle's voice and snapping fingers broke through my Lana-fogged mind.

I blinked him back into sight and sat straight. "Yeah, sorry, man. I got work shit on my mind," I said and went back to actually trying to listen to him talk about his trip to Milan.

He adjusted the sequin Santa hat on his blonde-tipped head and rolled his eyes. "Work shit, my ass. That was an I'm-in-love-with-Lana-but-she-dumped-my-ass look. You forget I've seen it for the past three days," he huffed, then slouched in his chair.

"I'm sorry that my unhappiness is so inconvenient for you. And she didn't dump me," I mumbled and dunked a fry in ketchup before tossing it back on my plate.

"First off, bitch, I never said your unhappiness was inconveniencing me." I went to argue, but Kyle held up a hand to stop me. "Second, you two slept together, so she did dump your ass."

I pinched the bridge of my nose, trying to stem the impending headache. "What exactly is your point?"

"My point is, stop trying to act like you're okay. You're not okay, and that's okay. You're in love with the girl, and she left. That shit is supposed to hurt. But what you do with it is what counts."

"What do you mean?"

"I mean, stop sending the chick gifts! You know Lana doesn't go for that, even if they're personalized to her. All she sees is you trying to buy her." He cocked his head as to say, "duh, dumbass," and that's precisely what I felt like. I always upheld how I didn't want a woman who wanted my money, and here I was practically throwing it at her in the form of gifts.

Leaning back in my chair, I ran a hand through my hair. "Damn, Kyle, you're right."

"I usually am, honey," he agreed flamboyantly, and as I sat and thought of my next step, I watched as people rushed by the café window to get out of the cold.

"Ugh, this pattern is just not working for me. I think I need a do-over," Kyle chattered on, and his last words had an idea coming to life in my head.

Turning my attention back to him, I asked, "What are you doing tonight, my friend?" and when he saw the mischievous smile break across my face, he shimmied his shoulders and claps.

"I am getting my man laid tonight," he hooted, and the entire café looked towards us.

"Okay, simmer down." I held up a hand. "One step at a time. Let's get Lana in the same room as me first." I took a drink of my beer. "Then we'll see where things go." I winked, and Kyle gave off another round of crowd-catching hoots.

❧ ⁂ ❧

We pulled up to Violet Delights at eleven PM sharp, and even though it was Christmas Eve, the line to get in stretched around the corner of the brightly lit club. Still, Kyle being a regular, had us passing up the line and heading straight into Kyle's VIP section.

A techno version of "Rockin' Around the Christmas Tree" thumped through the speakers as various Santas, Rudolphs, and even one guy dressed as baby Jesus was dancing merrily.

Kyle leaned over to speak into my ear. "The girls should already be here, so keep an eye out." I nodded in confirmation and began to look over the jolly crowd. My first pass came up empty, but when I scanned the crowd again, my eyes clung to the petite brunette in skin-tight red leather pants, matching red leather corset top with white fur trim, and a glittery Santa hat dancing in the middle of the dance floor. Her hands were in the air and a smile spread wide across her face as her blonde friend was grinding her ass against her.

Lana fanned her face and mimed getting a drink, and that was my cue. Standing, I rubbed my hands on my jeans to remove the clamminess. However, nothing could be done for the racing of my heart. Either this worked out, or it blew up in my face. At this point, I had nothing to lose, so with a steadying breath, I headed to the bar where I came to a stop right behind Lana, and as though she can feel my presence, she slowly turned. And fuck me running—my heart went from racing to near cardiac arrest. Her beautiful chocolate eyes latched onto mine, and her rose-red lips tipped up in the slightest smile.

I leaned into her, so she could hear me before speaking into her ear. "Hi, I'm James Kade." I pulled away and extended my hand for her to shake.

She bit her bottom lip and shook her head before taking my offered hand and lifting to her tip-toes to speak in my ear. "I'm Allana Mahue."

I nodded then leaned in again. "Would you like to go for a walk, Allana Mahue?" She looked out to the floor with a bright smile, and my eyes followed hers to find Lacey and Kyle smirking as they watched us. When Lana looked back at me, I gave her a dimpled smile and guided her to the coat check then out the front door.

We walked in silence for what seemed like hours when really it was only minutes. It was freezing, but Lana was enjoying the rare winter weather, so we walked.

"I forgive you, James." I stopped in my tracks and stared back at her, dumbfounded and thinking it couldn't be that easy. Then again, this was Lana we were talking about. My sweet, forgiving, gracious Lana.

"You do?" I asked and continued walking.

"I do. I did a lot of thinking and what you did was shitty, and I have never felt more betrayed." I winced at the sting her words caused but remained quiet. "And though I do not condone you lying, I understand the concern you had, and we became fast friends, so I'm sure it would have hurt regardless of whether you told me the truth a month down the road or six." She stopped and turned to me before bringing her chest to mine, her eyes narrowed. "But if you ever lie to me again, James Kade, I will pull your heart out through your penis. Got it?" she threatened, and a wide grin stretched my lips.

"Lacey give you that one?" I asked, and she growled at my lack of taking her seriously.

"Maybe, but it still stands." She pointed a finger in my face.

Catching her wrist, I brough her hand to lay over my heart, growing serious. "I swear to you, Allana, I will never lie to you again." I brushed the hair from her face and cupped her cheek. "I want you back. I want our friendship back. But I also want so much more. I want you as my best friend, my lover, my partner in crime." She giggled, and when a tear escaped her eye, I caught it with my thumb, "and one day as my wife. Because I love you, Lana." She gasped at my declaration, and before she could respond, I sealed my words with a kiss.

Pulling away, she placed her forehead against mine and gave me the words I'd been yearning to hear for six months. "I love you, James Kade." And as if heaven itself was celebrating, the sky opened up, and a flurry of fat snowflakes began to fall around us.

"Oh my God, James, it's snowing." Lana beamed in child-like wonder.

Looking at my watch, I smiled then cupped her cheeks. "It's 12:01," I said, and her eyes grew large with understanding.

"It's snowing on Christmas!" She jumped into my arms, and with a boisterous laugh, I spun us in a circle.

Her giggles floated on the frigid breeze, and when I stopped, I stared into her cocoa-colored eyes. "I am so damn glad I kissed you in the closet. Merry Christmas, Lana."

She rubbed the tip of her nose against mine. "Merry Christmas, James."

The End

The Twinks and the Harnessmaker

Leo Sparx

The little tourist town's unwavering winter sun set through the tall windows of the sex toy emporium I'd long since learned to call a novelty shop. Even with the mandatory darkened material lining the interior of most of the glass—meant to keep unmentionables from the eyes of unsuspecting pedestrians—the heat still radiated onto the white linoleum floor. In the penetrating rays, for a moment, I imagined what it may be like to live in a place with snow instead of sand. I wondered if it somehow made Christmas more magical.

In the last sparkle of light, body glitter glimmered from the twinky mannequins in the front display. To keep with decency ordinance, they wore apparel deemed more appropriate for onlookers than the jockstraps and thongs I'd dressed them in when we'd first opened. In their snug but modest briefs, the three life-sized dolls leaned on each other casually, the way old friends would over tropical cocktails or spiked eggnog.

No matter the season, the painted grins on their faces were forever frozen in a state of happiness, and while I flipped the plastic rainbow sign on the entrance from "Open" to "Closed" I thought about how long it had been since I'd smiled that way. Happiness was an emotion that had felt distant ever since the moment I realized our little business was doomed. With the invention of online shopping and its added discretion, no one was browsing for their butt plugs and double ended dildos in person anymore. It was inevitable. Unless we found a way to stop it, the naughty little shop we'd called home for two decades was going under.

I flipped on more lights and rummaged through a fresh shipment of padded trunks patterned with little trees and snowmen. With only a week until Christmas, I was a little behind the big chain stores who'd probably decorated their garment displays before Halloween. The holiday of sexy Santas and raunchy reindeer seemed to be coming earlier and earlier, but our customers seemed to be cumming, at least in our shop, less and less.

With the first mannequin's underwear at his ankles, my face was eye-level with the space between his thighs. An anatomically correct physique stared back at me. In a way, I was glad we'd paid extra for the thick shaft and generous handful of balls on all of them. Even flattened to their hard resin forms, they filled out anything I dressed them in perfectly.

Sometimes pulling boxers and speedos around their round ass cheeks made me hard, but this evening, it was the outline of a perfect uncut cock that made me adjust myself. The slim form with just the right amount of abs looked down at me with his static smile. I cleared my throat and felt the tip of my cock pushing at the inside of my pants.

Jeremy laughed behind me. "Worth it every time," he said, putting a hand on my shoulder. Bending down, he changed his voice to a whisper near my ear. "They turn me on sometimes, too."

I smiled and leaned my head onto his hairy knuckles. This place had been our dream come true for so long. We'd built every piece by hand, from the understated cockring wall to the tasteful gloryhole dressing rooms. From time to time, we even still made a lot of our own BDSM gear. Each harness we sold was handcrafted by us and tailored for various lifestyles and fetishes.

"Come to the backroom with me for a minute," Jeremy said, running his hand through my hair. His thumb circled the side of my neck and behind my earlobe.

"Let me dress them first," I said, preparing the elastic band to fit around the first man's hip bones. "You know the ice cream shop will report us if I leave them balls out." I tried to distract myself from Jeremy's sensual touching by sliding the candy cane underwear from the holiday collection under one of the mannequin's large bare feet, but he was persistent.

"They'll be fine for a little while." Jeremy smirked and reached for my hand. "Besides, this is work related. I have something that desperately needs your incredible attention to detail." He pulled me to my feet and grabbed around my waist, bringing me in close. While he ran his hand down the small of my back and into the top of my shorts, I could feel he was just as hard as I was.

Our apartment was nestled above our shop, but we both knew we wouldn't make it that far. Just through the saloon style doors to the storage area, my husband's mouth was on mine. Our lips clung to each other until Jeremy brought his hand down my shirt to release the buttons one at a time in rapid succession.

With my chest exposed, his fingers curved through the curly tendrils between my nipples, then pinched lightly at the sensitive areas. Erect to his liking, he moved his mouth over and around them. His tongue flicked and I threw my head back. After twenty years of marriage, he knew all of my weak spots.

When he went for my jeans, I let my palms rest on the workbench behind me. I thrust into his open mouth with my grasp around his head. Turning me around so he could rub his cock head on my hole and fuck me long and deep in the back of our failing business, I knew this was his way of helping me relieve stress. It was shorthand for letting me know, no matter what, we'd be okay.

Grabbing around my hips, he pulled me onto his thickness until I devoured him whole. I could feel his balls slapping against my cheeks and upper thighs, the pleasant sting of being on the receiving end of a generously hard pounding. While I white-knuckled the workbench laid out with harness materials, he slid his hand up my torso and to my throat. With a firm but gentle grip on my neck, he moaned loudly in my ear. He was going to cum soon.

I stroked at my dick using the salvia left behind by Jeremy's expert-level blowjob skills. Pushing my ass back on him while I pumped my cock, I wanted us to burst together.

"Here it comes, baby." The words escaped Jeremy's lips with a bearish growl. A few seconds later, I felt his warmth inside me while mine shot to the floor of the workshop. I relaxed my body and leaned my weight on the workbench. Still buried deep within me, Jeremy rested his beard on my shoulder. I could feel the sticky hair between us and smell the sweat of an intense sexual workout.

I should have been tired. I should have followed my husband up the steps to our home when he dismounted and helped me clean up the mess we'd made. Instead, I kissed him goodnight and buckled my pants. I arranged the materials on the workbench, prepared to use what little of the expensive materials I had left to make a few more harnesses.

Jeremy's attempt at calming me had helped, but the look he'd had in his eyes while he ascended the stairs without me stuck in my head. Disappointment, sure, but there was something more. A sadness about seeing something we both loved so much come to close. And while I was certain he respected my dedication to using every moment I had to save the store, we both knew it was futile. That was the emotion that sat between his forehead and chin. It was knowing our ship was going down and watching me try to bail us out with a teaspoon.

I smashed my rubber mallet lightly on the grommets between the straps of colorful fabric. Leather wasn't the standard when it came to fetish gear anymore, but quality synthetic textile came with a hefty price tag, and right now, we couldn't afford it.

Still, I trimmed and stitched with what I had. Next to my worn fingers from two decades of making BDSM apparel, the industrial sewing machine whirred, and my riveter made contact with the constellation of silver circles connecting the carefully measured pieces. When people did come in to do some shopping, no one seemed to understand the amount of time it took to make even one harness by hand. But whether they sold or not, I was determined to finish three before the store opened the next day.

Half of my face felt warm when I woke up cheek-down on the workbench. Somehow, I'd fallen asleep mid-composition. Not one of the harnesses was even close to done. I rubbed my eyes then pushed the cut straps and shiny buttons away with frustration. Maybe Jeremy was right. Maybe it was time for me to stop trying to save our emporium. If the tourists didn't want our queer little shop here anymore, perhaps it was time to give up.

Hitting the lights in the front of the store, darkness covered the dildo corner and inflatable butt plug spindle. It swallowed the condom bowls and case of lubricants. Even the rotating display of poppers and body glitter disappeared into blackness.

Sighing, I left the sad scene behind and climbed the steps until I found my husband cuddled in bed. I took off my clothes and spooned his warm naked body. As I curled into him, he reached back to pat my bare ass. He turned over and kissed me softly while his partial hardness rubbed at my inner thigh. I smiled, wondering if he was going to try to get a second round out of me but then something hit me.

"The mannequins!" I said, louder than I'd meant to. "I never finished re-dressing them!"

Jeremy let out a sleepy laugh. "They'll be okay until morning."

I started to get out of bed. "You know the neighbors are going to complain about—"

He pulled me in close, back to the comfort of our shared bed. "Let them. Give them something to talk about. Once we're gone, the legend of the well-endowed mannequins will just have to be our legacy." Jeremy smiled and nuzzled into my shoulder.

It wasn't the legacy I wanted to leave behind, but he was right. They could wait one night. I'd be up in the morning to slide on the candy cane, snowflake, and reindeer briefs over their round little ass cheeks. If a few early birds on the boardwalk sent complaints to the zoning officials, so be it. We were on our way

out anyway. In the meantime, I was going to stay in bed with my husband and enjoy what I was certain would be our last holiday in our home.

Most days, I didn't mind being woken up with a good bang, but I preferred it not to be the kind on my door before the start of business. The harsh sound of rapid knocking echoed up the stairway and directly to our bedroom.

Jeremy turned to his side. "Absolutely do not answer that."

While he covered his face with a pillow, I grabbed my housecoat and tied it while I stumbled down the stairs to the shop. The tail of the flowy silk robe followed behind me until I reached the front entrance. On the other side was a man I'd never seen before, urgency splattered on his face. He pounded his fist against the glass, shaking the rusted copper bells attached to the top. Even when he saw me reaching to unlock the door, he didn't stop.

I shook my head quickly and rubbed my face, attempting to wake up and find the words to apologize for the mannequins I was certain he was about to tell me were obscene and highly offensive. While I unlocked the deadbolts, I tongued the corners of my mouth, hoping to look as presentable as possible. It wasn't until I peeked my head through the opening that he finally ceased his knocking.

"I need to talk to you about your window display immediately!" he yelled. The sun couldn't have been up for more than a few hours, and here was this stranger demanding interaction from me before the dew had even dried from the boardwalk.

"Are you from the council?" I asked calmly, clearing the nighttime frog from my throat. "Give me a few minutes, and I'll cover the mannequins up."

"Cover them up? No! Take all three of those harnesses off of them because I'm buying them all!" The stranger thrust his way through the doorway and while I looked on with confusion, he made his way to the twinky forms in the front window. "I can't wait to get my hands on them!"

I glanced at the mannequin's backsides. Not only were they wearing the holiday patterns I'd laid out for them but also the matching red, green, and white harnesses I could have sworn I'd abandoned the night before. They looked incredible.

"Do these distinguished gentlemen have names?" the man asked with an enthusiastic grin.

Glancing at the only identifiable markings the identical mannequins possessed, I felt inclined to improvise. If only for the sale. The only thing that made them different from each other was the design of their new underwear. "Well, I suppose for now they're Candy Cane, Snowflake, and Reindeer."

The stranger nodded, apparently satisfied with my answer.

Still in just my housecoat, I reached into the display and released the clips fastened across each of the men's chests. The grommets and rivets were expertly laid. Somehow, I had achieved better craftsmanship than I had been capable of in years, and I didn't even remember doing it. With one of the mannequins resting in my arms as I undid his front straps, his constant smile caught my eye. Perhaps I was still half-asleep, but his expression seemed even more gleeful. The eyes of the mannequin recently named Candy Cane sparkled at me.

"Whatever they cost, it doesn't matter. I've never seen anything made so perfectly." The stranger said, holding the tagless merchandise in his hand. "As a matter of fact..." His voice trailed off while he set a briefcase I hadn't realized he was carrying near the register.

He wasn't wearing the typical getup for a beach tourist. Instead of flip flops and board shorts, he was in dress slacks and tie. He pulled out a long wallet embossed with initials and an expensive looking metal pen. Licking the tip of the ballpoint, he flipped open what appeared to be a checkbook and began scribbling.

"How many can I get you to make for me in every color for this much?" The well-dressed stranger tore out the rectangular page and handed it over. A number with more zeros than we'd seen in our bank account since opening the store stared back at me in wet ink.

I stood silent in disbelief while the man looped the three harnesses around his inner-elbow. "However many you can do. I trust your judgement. I'll be back next week for the rest."

Before I could say another word, the old copper bells looped to the top of the front door jingled. The man was gone. A week from today. Christmas morning.

I hadn't even bothered to switch the sign to "Open" when I dragged my heavy feet up the stairs again. The multiple zeros stuck between my thumb and index finger, I still couldn't believe what I was looking at. In the house, Jeremy stood over the bathroom sink, brushing his teeth. Without a word, I handed him the check and sat on the side of the tub. I looked down at my corduroy slippers, still not certain I wasn't dreaming.

Paper in hand, Jeremy wedged the bamboo handle toothbrush into his cheek and turned off the water. He stared at the numbers before spitting into the sink and tossing the toothbrush to the side and wiping his mouth. "Guessing here but ... someone complained, and you felt so bad that you blew them, and this is the generous tip for your service?"

I shook my head.

"Don't underestimate your skills, babe." Jeremy laughed. He obviously thought the check was a joke.

"We've got an order. A big order." I was still looking at my shoes. "But it wasn't my services." Looking up at my husband, he suddenly seemed concerned. I sighed. "Have you ever seen me sleepwalk? Or sleep ... work?"

There was a pause between us while Jeremy tilted his head in confusion. "I'm apparently going to need a cup of coffee for this," he said with a smile.

Over two steaming mugs, I explained to my husband that I didn't remember finishing the harnesses. Not only that, but the detail and quality looked better than my stuff had in at least ten years.

With the giant check sitting between us at the kitchen table, Jeremy reached out a paw and curled it into mine. "We're just getting old, babe." He squeezed my hand affirmingly until I looked into his eyes. "If there's any silver lining though, it sounds like your sudden sleep disorder just put us back in business. We better get to work."

I smiled back, but I still wasn't sure how I had accomplished such intricate work. Even so, nothing was going to stop me from putting this money in the bank and buying quality materials.

After a shopping spree, yards of thick fabric and piles of polished metal rings were sprawled out across the entire backroom. Jeremy measured, I cut, and we both laid out the designs for more harnesses than we'd ever produced.

The stranger hadn't specified, so we did a collection of styles. H-Style with a dangling hoop that could be easily attached to a leash or pulled for momentum. A standard 4-Strap that wrapped around the shoulders and accentuated the nipples. The Y-Harness came with two holding points at the sternum and stomach that could easily be attached to a cockring with an added single strap.

And while the Sling-type was the easiest to put on because it sat like a jacket, it was the Gladiator-style that offered the most flash. It took less materials and only hung by one shoulder strap, but it sent a message. The message that whoever was wearing it was absolutely ready to fuck. It was the style I'd chosen for Candy Cane, the mannequin with the sparkling eyes.

Six days later, the shop had opened and closed like every other day that year. Minimal customers looking for the same Homo Happy Meal: a condom, single pellet of lube, and a petite bottle of mild poppers. We knew that somewhere under the boardwalk, the hustlers and tourists were meeting up and exchanging fluids for paper money, but we saw them less and less. Off-season or not, our small town's very own Dick Dock was not a consistent source of income.

Luckily for us, the stranger's check had cleared, but while we'd been working nonstop since his arrival, there was no way I would have enough product ready for him by the following day. As I hunched over the workbench hammering grommets and slipping carefully constructed loops through rings, I worried that even with the new materials I was able to afford, my speed would never match my magical sleepwalking night. Which unfortunately had never happened again.

Buried in a pile of unfinished work, I worried about what would happen the next day when the man came in for his order. I wondered if he would scoff at what my aging hands were able to accomplish in 168 hours. If he would request we return his money, leaving us back where we started, or worse, drowning in costs for merchandise we would never sell.

"Come to bed, please," Jeremy said from the bottom of the steps. "We've done everything we can. It's just going to have to be enough." His flannel pajamas were open at the fly, exposing his pubic hair and the top of his cock.

I nodded at the opening and smiled. "That for me?"

Jeremy looked down at his fly and laughed. It didn't seem to have been intentional, but he still tugged at it and shimmied his hips back and forth with a smirk. "It is if you're hungry for it."

Truth was, I was exhausted, but I could never turn him down. I cleaned up and hit the lights in the workshop to follow him upstairs. Immediately on my knees, I took him in my mouth and sucked him from tip to base, cupping his balls and licking the delicate skin.

After he pulled my shirt over my head, I reached for his nipples and playfully twisted. I grabbed a generous helping of one of his ass cheeks and squeezed. Straddling him on the bed, I rode around his hips and bounced slowly back and forth, teasing him with my tight hole and letting his head barely find its way inside before pulling back. He moaned every time I moved away while he ran his hands up my chest.

Finally ready to take all of him, I reached for the bottle of lube on our nightstand and flipped the cap. A few drops had already fallen onto my palm when I heard the floorboards creak. We both froze mid-position. "What was that?" Jeremy whispered.

With the slippery lube half-squeezed in my hand, we listened. The floor creaked again then a small bang followed. It sounded like my rubber mallet down below our apartment. I looked at my husband with eyes that said, "Is there something in the house?" Before I could articulate my thoughts, someone giggled.

Jeremy sat up quickly, unintentionally tossing me to the other side of the bed. "Oh, that's fucking creepy," he said more loudly.

Close behind my husband, we descended the stairs one step at a time. On the bottom landing, we peeked around the corner, expecting to see intruders or something more sinister. Instead, we saw three plump asses bent over the pile of tools and materials. They were fixing my work and making new harnesses. An entire rack of them on individual hangers hung pristine and ready to be sold.

With my tools in their hands, the figures turned and spotted us. The lifeless smiles and chiseled bodies that normally stood silent in our display window were not only standing in my workshop, they were moving and working. Their faces had somehow turned to something more human and handsome. Their skin was no longer made from a mix of plastic, resin, and wood.

While they stood staring at us in their tight briefs, we pulled back around the corner. All three mannequins giggled as soon as we were out of view. I looked back at Jeremy who was rubbing his eyes. My disbelief matched his. There was no way this was real. I was sleepwalking again, or we both were. We'd both had too much coffee trying to complete the order—that was it.

Jeremy pressed his back to the wall and whispered again. "Answer me honestly. Are the hot mannequins out there using the sewing machine?"

Before I could answer, one of the twinks popped their head into the stairwell. We jumped back. He didn't talk but extended his hand in a friendly way and motioned for us to follow. In what still felt like a hallucination, we both took a deep breath, then rose to join the trio in the backroom.

Surrounded by a sea of packaged sex toys and restraints, the mannequins circled us like adorable sharks. They smiled but still didn't speak. With their work complete and their tools abandoned, the twinks tugged on the growing bulges. The one with the candy cane patterned briefs pulled the elastic band down under his balls to let his thick cock flop in front of us. Snowflake and Reindeer followed his lead then reached over to stroke each other.

Jeremy and I had managed to slip on short trunks before sneaking down the steps, but soon the boys were close and pulling at them. A hand reached for my hardness. Candy Cane flicked at the head of my cock and parted his lips. He kneeled below me, and with his eyes focused on mine, took me deep. Surprisingly, the mouth that had seemed so rigid before was now soft, warm, and wet.

His tongue was welcoming and his throat endless as he swallowed my length over and over again. Next to me, Snowflake and Reindeer kissed my husband's chest and licked at his nipples. As a duo, they made their way to his cock and sucked at the pre-cum dripping from him. They swallowed and caressed him softly, milking every drop of clear slippery liquid.

From the corner of my eye, I watched them each bend in front of him with their tight underwear pulled just below their ass cheeks. Jeremy stoked himself and looked my way for approval. Even if this was a dream, consent from all parties was important. I nodded.

While I heard him crack open the plastic seal on a new bottle of lube, Candy Cane grabbed me by the waist and lowered me to the ground next to him. My head was in his lap immediately, taking his thickness as far as I could in my mouth. The dick and balls I'd gotten used to seeing as half-flattened were now in full 3D and pulsing on my tongue.

From behind me, Snowflake and Reindeer moaned, and I saw more toys falling like a blizzard from a nearby box. Vibrating plugs and prostate massagers, all ready to fill the holes I wasn't even aware the mannequins had. Jeremy was right—we really had gotten our money's worth.

Candy Cane pushed me lightly by the shoulders and put me on my side. His uncut cock seemed to be hand-carved to perfection but still smooth and fleshy. With one of my legs lifted slightly, he rubbed the head over my hole enough times to prepare me then slid gently inside. He thrust back and forth, moving me in his desired rhythm by my waist. His fingers traveled up my stomach and chest until they reached my mouth. I sucked them as he fucked me.

Moving to my hands and knees, Candy Cane got behind me and pounded my hole more rapidly. From my new position, I watched Jeremy sliding bulbous plugs into one of the boys while he pumped inside the other. He switched back and forth while they yelped with pleasure. Between Candy Cane's thick cock and watching my husband do what I knew he did best, my dick was drizzling onto the workshop floor.

I felt something new slide inside me. Something round and firm. Another followed. Then one more. By the time my brain caught up with my body, I realized I had an entire string of anal beads in me. Seemingly pleased with how much I'd devoured, Candy Cane pulled them out slowly, one ball at a time. I bit my lip as each one popped out. More of my pre-cum puddled as the twink moved in front of me and motioned for me to stand.

With all of us in the center of the workshop, we stroked together. I pumped hard and fast at my cock while I watched the men I'd always thought of as inanimate objects jerk their heavy dicks. Jeremy reached for me as we all began to cum and looped his pinky finger into mine. We came together furiously, then collapsed to the ground. We'd left a mess of opened clamshell packages, lube overflow, and sperm that I was too tired to think about cleaning. With a full load expelled, I closed my eyes and fell asleep.

A single ray of light through the blackout material near the front entrance woke me followed by a familiar banging on the door. When I looked around, I saw Jeremy. He was sitting with his back against the workbench, fully clothed. Somehow, even though I couldn't remember going upstairs, I was dressed too. Not only was everything spotless, but the remaining materials had been turned into even more harnesses. However, there was no sign of the twinks. The hot mannequins and their remarkable work ethic has disappeared. Candy Cane, Snowflake, and Reindeer were gone. Only their briefs, folded neatly into a stack, had been left behind.

On our feet, we both ran for the front door. The mysterious man who had left us the large check pushed his way inside again. "Merry Christmas! I see you're letting the gentlemen take it easy for the holiday. No fetish gear?" he asked with a smile, nodding at the display window. There they were, the magical twinks in their usual positions, leaning on each other and frozen in time.

"In any case, have you finished?" the man asked, looking back at us.

Jeremy cleared his throat. "Oh yeah, we finished last night alright."

I shook my head at his joke but kept an eye on the mannequins. My first instinct was that it had definitely been a dream, but Jeremy clearly remembered. Not only that, but in the back room, there were still racks filled with incredible gear that I knew I hadn't completed on my own. Something mystical had happened in our little shop.

We wheeled the merchandise carts out one at a time, and the man inspected the work. "Truly exquisite and worth every penny." He smiled. "That of course was a down payment before. I'll write you a check for the rest now."

The rest?

Jeremy and I glanced at each other, but neither of us spoke. While the businessman jotted a new number into his checkbook, we loaded his purchases and offered him complimentary lube and popper samples. He politely declined.

When the door closed behind him and the old bells steadied, we sprinted to the mannequins. We tried to talk to them, to ask them what we had done to deserve such a delightful Queermas miracle, but there was no reply. The trio's eyes and smiles had returned to their one-dimensional default setting. Under their holiday briefs, the impressive packages were no longer soft to the touch.

"I think I need a nap now," Jeremy said, rubbing his temples. "Let's not open up today."

Looking at the twinks in the window, I wanted to find a way to thank them for everything they had done. I wanted to give them a gift like they had for us. "Help me with something first," I said.

We spent the rest of the afternoon cutting and measuring, stretching and sewing, until we finally had three completed outfits. All these years they had done so much for us to model our latest arrivals and styles. Now, they had clothes of their own. Clothes they could keep.

We dressed them lovingly while the sun set through the windows of our little store. The way the rays shone and glittered on the polished white linoleum made me smile. Snow or not, this place and this man were Christmas to me. Knowing our shop and home would survive another few years—that was the best gift of all.

When we finally called it a night, Jeremy held me in his arms as we talked about the strange orgy and what we would do in the future if the money ever ran out. With a tight hug, he said the only words I needed to hear: "As long as we're together."

The shop was our baby, sure, but it wasn't our love. Maybe it was the holiday that made it easier to see that the strength of our relationship mattered more than any sex toys or handcrafted harnesses ever would.

A few hours after passing out next to my husband, I heard the bells of the front door jingle. Down the steps in my housecoat and slippers, I saw the empty display window. Before the mannequin twinks were completely out of sight, Candy Cane turned to me with his sparkling eyes and winked.

I smiled back and waved goodbye, knowing that we would never see them again. In that moment I knew what had occurred between the five of us wasn't something I would ever be able to explain, but it was exactly the kind of miracle I needed to believe in Christmas magic.

Home Free

Jean Bex

"Hold still, darlin'. This will only take a sec." Nancy's words were slightly garbled, her mouth precariously balancing a handful of pushpins as her hands carefully folded back the seam along my satin-covered waist.

I tried desperately to muffle my sigh. I had been standing for what seemed like hours on the tiny wooden stool our mother Stella always used for her home tailoring business. Now that her widow's hands were riddled with arthritis, the stool resided under the guest room bed most of the time. Nancy and her husband Rick had moved into the farmhouse the year after Daddy passed, Nancy taking over management of the milking and Rick commuting the two hours each day to his job as a state trooper. Mom was content to take charge of the family's meals and laundry. According to my sister, she often retired to the bedroom she once shared with my father immediately following supper, speaking very little to her eldest daughter and son-in-law, but when I phoned to announce the good news, she seemed to spring to life again, chatting happily with Nancy about flower choices and china patterns. When I arrived from the airport the day before, I was greeted at the door by Mom holding out the wedding dress she had pulled from storage.

"None of that, now," Nancy said, her voice clearer now that the last pin was securely fastened at my spine. "You know she's been waiting for this since you were a teenager. It was just my dumb luck to get a body like dad's side of the family." Nancy was at least six inches taller than me: broader-shouldered, but not brawny or mannish by any means. Her frame also boasted plentiful curves, something nearly absent from my silhouette. I was small-boned with narrow hips and small but pert breasts that rarely if ever necessitated a bra. Jacob, my boyfriend since college, always told me that he liked my figure, but then again, we rarely made love with the lights on. Even after he proposed last month, as I slipped into his bedroom wearing the sheer babydoll I'd saved for a special occasion, he switched off the nightstand lamp as soon as I climbed into bed next to him.

I smirked. "I know. I'm sorry. I'm just tired, I guess. Between the flight yesterday and trying to sleep last night in the total silence... how do you *do* it? How did *I* do it my whole childhood? It feels like I'm lying in a vacuum: pitch dark and no car engines, no voices, nothing!" It was rare for me to return to the farm, even on holidays like these, something I admit to feeling a bit guilty about but not enough to change. I always made up some excuse: the plane fare was too expensive, the university was offering an intersession seminar I wanted to attend, I'd be home for the next break: I promised. The truth is, I fell in love with the city: the constant motion of the crowds, the fluorescent glow of the lights, and the unending hum of the traffic lulled me to sleep each evening. On the farm, as I lay in bed last night, I saw nothing but black sky dotted with stars outside the guest room's window and heard only the wind through the grass and an occasional bird or cricket. It seemed almost maddening, and I wondered how I managed to have gotten any rest for my first eighteen years.

Nancy stepped back and looked at me from head to toe. "Okay," she said. "You can take a look. It shouldn't take me but a day or so to stitch it. As long as you give me a hand with my regular duties, I should have it ready before Jake arrives." She offered me a hand and I gingerly stepped down to the floor. "Sunday, right?"

I walked over to the standing mirror next to the window and pulled my shoulders back. The semi-transparent trim on the dress's neckline delicately tickled my collarbone. I let my fingertips run along the edge, smoothing the lace. It was soft, not scratchy like it appeared to be.

"He's coming Sunday, right?" Nancy repeated. "Julia?"

I removed my finger from my neck. "Yeah... yes. He has some sort of work thing Saturday. He said he'd be on the first flight in the morning." Monday was Christmas. It would be the first holiday Jacob would spend with my family; by this time next year, we'd host our own festivities in the city. I reached back to unhook the bodice, but Nancy jumped suddenly in my direction.

"Hold on, there," she said. "Let me help. This clasp is a bitch."

I stood patiently until I felt the material loosen, then I let the dress fall softly down and stepped carefully out from it. The sun streaming through the window felt good on my bare chest, and I hesitated before walking over to retrieve my t-shirt. It was one of those picturesque early winter days where the unseasonably mild temperatures and smell of the bare earth warming could trick the mind into thinking it was springtime. I let my eyes wander along the edge of the barn and down to the road. Two of the cows were languidly nuzzling something on the ground near the fence. I looked slowly back toward the barn. A young, broad-shouldered man in a faded worksheet and jeans was walking around the corner, grasping a tightly packed bale of hay between two gloved hands. He tossed it on the ground out of sight, then brushed his hands on his thighs.

"Mom didn't tell me you hired a ranch hand," I said, my eyes still on the stranger below until he disappeared out of sight again.

Nancy stood next to me and looked out. "You mean Thomas?" She glanced over the fields, then backed away, rearranging the wedding dress on the cloth-covered mannequin. "Yeah, with Rick gone all day and Mom … out of commission most days, I just couldn't keep up with everything without some help. He's pretty much taken over the cattle, and I'm grateful, to be honest." She paused, then smiled. "And he's not bad to look at either, that's for certain."

No, he was not. *Thomas.* From above, it was hard to tell the exact color of his eyes, but they were lighter than his tanned skin. When he appeared again from behind the barn, he was carrying his hat in one hand and running a gloveless hand through his dark brown hair with the other. Puffs of warm breath smoked in front of his mouth. Something must have grazed his face because he waved his hat to shoo it, but as he did, he spied the pale-skinned woman gazing down at him from the second story window.

I could see the change in his expression as he realized I was topless, and though every instinct in my bones was pushing me to step back and cover myself, I remained fixed at the pane. When he looked back, we locked eyes. I ran my hand from the place where the lace had been just a moment before down to my navel, pausing purposefully at my nipple to caress it slightly. Thomas placed his hat against his chest and watched me intently, his eye widening in appreciation. Then, realizing what I was doing, I felt my cheeks blush and I smiled conspiratorially before walking away to get dressed.

Nancy placed her hand on my shoulder. "I'm so glad you're home, even if it's just for the holidays," she said.

I smoothed an imaginary wrinkle out of the top of my jeans. I was glad, too. As we walked out of the room together, I stole a glance out the window.

Thomas was gone.

The next morning, the weather had shifted, and this urgent nudge at the rapidly approaching frigid months prompted me to dig out an old flannel shirt. I was glad for Jacob's absence: even the soft, thick material couldn't disguise my nipples as they stood at attention in the chill, and Jake would have balked at such a public display.

Rick left for his shift in the early dawn, and Nancy was taking my mother to the market in town. "Any requests?" she asked before ducking her head into the car. I shook my head, then watched the blue sedan as it backed down the long, dirt driveway and disappeared along the road and out of sight.

That morning, I had watched Thomas surreptitiously from the pantry window. Although he tried to disguise it, I watched him glance hopefully up at the empty guest room more than once. As soon as Nancy's car was out of sight, I grabbed a knit hat from the mudroom, slipped into onto my head, and walked swiftly to the barn. Although I don't think he noticed when I pushed open the door and slipped quietly behind him, he didn't seem startled when I called out his name.

"Thomas?" I said loudly, the word sounding clipped and smothered in the dim, relatively warm air of the closed space. "I'm Julia. I'm Nancy's sister." I held out my hand for him to shake.

Thomas's eyes danced a beat. He walked closer to me and accepted my hand in his, held it for longer than was expected. "It's nice to meet you, ma'am," he said. "Nancy talks about you a lot. You moved to the city, right? For school?"

I slid my hand slowly out from his, tracing my fingers along the rough patches on his palm as I did. "Yeah," I said. "I never quite made it home after graduation, I suppose."

Thomas removed his hat and placed it on a nearby hale bale. He ran his hand through his hair. I could see a smattering of dirt that had attached itself from the air to the sweat on his cheek and felt an overwhelming urge to touch it, not to brush it away but to smear it deeper into his skin. "I tried it out myself for a few years," he admitted, smiling. "You don't notice the quiet until you've been away from it for a while."

I smiled. "You understand."

Thomas rocked back and forth on his boots. "You must be going a little stir-crazy, being back here."

I let my eyes wander along his body. He wasn't too tall, but Thomas was certainly not short. His stomach was flat, but his arms bulged through the fabric of his shirt insistently.

Feeling my assessment, he glanced shyly at the ground, then tipped his head toward me: a practiced look, I was certain, one that he knew gave him the instant appearance of a naughty schoolboy. I wondered how many women he had charmed with it. Then, I decided if I was going to be one of them, I would react differently than most of them surely had. I stepped closer to him and placed my hand on his face, rubbing the dirt upward gently with the side of my index finger. Up close, the smell of him, of grass and earth mingled with a hint of soap, was something primal and nourishing at the same time.

He glanced about the barn, then met my eyes again. "It's awfully warm around here for Christmas, don't you think?" He smiled, his mouth crooking up on only one side of his face.

I smiled back. "I don't know about that. New England can be funny that way. Some years, we get a freak storm in October. Others, the ground isn't white until New Year's."

We were both silent for a long moment. Then, I watched his eyes as they softened, and without another word, Thomas reached forward and wrapped his arms around my waist to pull me close, bringing his mouth to mine. The kiss was raw and urgent, yet careful, as if Thomas were gorging himself with a savory meal and did not want to spill even a crumb. I let myself melt into his embrace but aggressively kissed him back. I wasn't going to be the girl who was taken: I would be the one to take.

As his arms relaxed, his hands slid around to the front of my jeans. His palms were wide, and his fingers grasped my hips firmly; his thumbs spread outward, rubbing the tops of my thighs softly. I pulled my lips from his and unbuttoned my shirt, forcing my eyes to remain on Thomas's face. His eyes flickered toward my mouth, then down to my breasts. Before I could move closer, he leaned his head down to my chest and pressed his mouth softly around my nipple. The warmth of his cheek radiated onto my skin, and he began to suck gently, his tongue tracing circles that made me shiver.

As his hands fumbled along the waist of my jeans, finally unbuttoning and unzipping them, I pushed him away once more, this time with more urgency.

"I'm sorry, Miss Julia… did I—" He looked at me in disappointment, but as I hooked my thumbs into my waistband and pushed my pants and panties down to my knees, his expression changed to one of serious concentration. I excitedly turned my back and bent over to lie forward onto the stack of hay bales, presenting my ass to him.

Thomas did not hesitate. I heard him fumble with his own jeans, then felt the tip of his cock pressing insistently along the back of my thighs and between my cheeks, his fingers exploring me. He wanted to take his time. We had all the time in the world, as far as I was concerned. I knew I was already ready, the persistent longing to feel him inside me pulsing, grasping hold of my rational thought as it grew more and more insistent. His hands drifted slowly back to my hips, but this time, his thumbs tickled the back of my thighs. He traced the curve of my ass, then urgently spread my legs wide.

I braced myself against the hay, the faded yellow autumn smell filling my nose and lulling me like a drug. The grit of his stubble rubbed playfully against the inside of my thighs, then my cheeks. His mouth was hot and wet as his tongue explored me, licking every inch and wiggling into me. The rollercoaster of orgasm began its slow ascent up to the top of the drop, and I pushed myself back against his face to drive him forward. He obliged, curling his tongue up in a hard, stroking motion.

It was then that we heard the car door slam.

"No, no..." I whispered, silently cursing whoever had decided to come home early. I was so close...

Thomas pulled back, and I stood up, turned around, and wriggled my jeans back up to my waist. I began to speak, but Thomas put his finger to his lips. We listened silently to the soft patter of footsteps walking away, toward the house. Still, Thomas zipped up his pants and walked apologetically to me. "I should be working; I'm so sorry, Miss Julia," he said.

His eyes were still glazed with lust as he said it, but I quickly buttoned my shirt. "Too bad you don't have any vacation days saved up," I said, smiling.

He placed his hand on the side of my face and stroked it softly. "I am free tomorrow afternoon. Would you like to go into town, maybe get some lunch?"

I laid my hand on his and gently pulled it away. "I'd like to see you, but I'd like to stay here, if that's alright? How about I come get you after lunch?"

He smiled and squeezed my hand. I slipped out of the barn and back up the stairs of the house before he could say no.

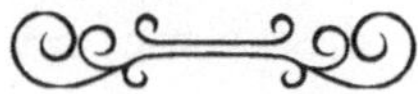

That evening, the mall was mobbed, swarms of procrastinated shoppers desperate to finalize their gift lists before the weekend madness. Nancy and I walked slowly, arm in arm within the bustling crowd, our jackets draped through the straps of our handbags and the growing warmth from the hordes of people making it feel like summer.

Nancy stopped suddenly and wrapped her hand around my wrist, staring into a nearby window. "Oh yes," she said. "This—this is the one." She pulled me into the store. Despite the short distance between the retail space and the sweltering hallway, the atmosphere immediately felt ten degrees cooler. I looked around. We were in a lingerie shop, one of those high-priced boutiques with soft lighting and model-beautiful salesclerks.

"Nan," I whispered, "I can't afford anything in here. I have a florist, and invitation printers, and God knows what else to pay for—"

But my sister had already detached herself from me and was sliding hangers carefully around a circular rack, eyeing the collection of silk chemises, then moving on to a display against the wall. "And I still have to buy you something drop dead sexy for your honeymoon, since you refuse to let me throw you a bachelorette party." She pulled out a semi-sheer teddy and held it in front of me. "Try this one," she instructed and resumed her perusal.

I glanced around the sales floor. I didn't see a sign for a dressing room. "Where?" I stage whispered.

Nancy pulled out another item and thrust it in my direction. She nodded toward the rear of the store. "It's in the back, by the register," she said, then moved onto to another rack.

Before she could push anything else into my hand, I wandered in the direction of her instruction. Sure enough, there was a doorway covered by a heavy velvet curtain, an impossibly tall woman standing in front of it. She escorted me inside, placing the two hangers delicately on silver hooks.

Hurriedly, I lay my bag and coat on the upholstered chair and slipped my blouse over my chest. I pushed my boots off without bothering to untie them, then unbuttoned and pushed my jeans to my ankles. I paused. The image of Thomas drinking in my naked body just hours earlier flashed through my mind.

I stepped out of the jeans and stood in front of the full-length mirror, watching my own reflection as I slipped my feet into the leg holes of the first item and pulled it carefully along my thong and the halter portion, over my head. The fabric was smooth, cool, a rich burgundy like a glass of merlot. I ran my hands along my waist, sliding them down to the tops of my thighs.

I turned around and looked back at myself in the mirror again. The dramatic cut of the lingerie left my back completely bare. Spontaneously, I reached my arms up and rested them against the fabric-covered wall of the stall, watching my shoulder muscles tense and lengthen in the doppelgänger across from me, the curve of my ass peeking out from the silk bottoms. Thomas. I remembered the slight scratchiness of his cheek against the inside of my thigh.

I unhooked the strap from around my neck and let the fabric slide over my nipples and down to my stomach. Keeping one arm pressed against the divider,

I reached my other hand into the front of my panties. The tip of my forefinger pushed urgently against my clit, and I pressed harder, a slow rhythm, and bent my body forward. Thomas was behind me, against me, inside me, the small patch of soft dark hair on his lower stomach rubbing against the top of my ass.

I pushed the teddy to the floor and turned around, leaning back against the wall. My twin did the same. My swollen clit held captive between my index and middle fingers, I gently squeezed, slowly moving my hand up and down. My thong was damp, the delicious friction almost too much to bear. In the mirror, my thigh muscles clenched, then relaxed.

"Do you need another size or style?" The lithe salesclerk's voice drifted suddenly over the stall's heavy door.

I stopped moving my hand but did not remove it. "No, I think I have what I need," I said, trying to keep my voice as even as possible. If the clerk was inquiring, Nancy would be soon as well. I wiped my hand on the front of my panties and laughed softly to myself as I frantically redressed and rifled through my purse for a hand wipe.

Sure enough, a moment later, Nancy pulled the door open without warning and stuck her head inside. "I found three others if you're not in love with those," she said.

"No, no," I protested, trying my best to gracefully slide the burgundy silk back onto the hanger. "I like this one, and it fits well. If you're sure…"

"I'm sure, and I'm glad—someone just said it's beginning to snow. We should boogie if we want to make it home before it gets too slippery," she said, walking back toward the velvet curtain.

"The first snow of the year, just in time for Santa," I noted as I followed her out to the register. "I guess it's better late than never."

Late Saturday morning, I found myself alone in the house once again. My mother absconded to town, this time, to browse mother-of-the-bride dresses with some of the ladies she met for breakfast after church each week. Nancy and Rick had departed early to attend a friend's holiday luncheon but assured me they'd find a way to escape after the gifts were unwrapped. Outside, the sky was blue and bright, and I slipped out of my pajamas to stand naked in the warmth of the sun again. In my apartment in the city, I was wary to do anything near one of my two windows after catching a man in the building across the street pointing a camera lens my way a week after I moved in. The city was a constant source of interesting adventures, but it was void of truly private moments.

I walked closer to the window and pressed my body against the glass, its coolness icing my nipples and the skin on the soft rounding of my tummy just beneath my belly button. As I backed slightly away, I ran my hands along the smooth tops of my thighs.

I knew without looking that he'd be there.

Sure enough, Thomas stood in front of the barn, still holding the hammer he'd carried back from fixing a blemish in the fence. He rested it on the ground in front of the door, still tipped with the remnants of the previous evening's dusting, and crossed his arms in front of his chest, playfully gazing up at me with a mischievous grin. He nodded his head as if to stay, "Continue."

As much as I wanted to engage in a peep show fantasy, I knew that our time alone was limited, so I beckoned with my hand for him to join me upstairs. He looked down at the ground, his grin widening to an enormous smile, then back up to me again before jogging quickly to the back door, out of my line of sight.

His heavy footsteps echoed almost immediately in the hall. "I've never been up here," he said hesitantly, poking his head into the guest room. "You sure this is okay?"

"It's more than okay," I said, walking over to the still unmade bed. "Take off your clothes," I added softly.

He unbuttoned his shirt and peeled it from his torso. The tan I'd spotted on his face and neck continued down to his waist. I imagined him walking shirtless around the farm all summer, the hot sun bronzing his body. He kicked off his boots and pushed his jeans and boxer shorts down to the floor, stepping out of them with surprising grace. As he walked over to me, he was already erect. "Miss Julia—" he began.

I ran my hands over his chest, feeling the soft down of hair undulate under my palms. The muscles visibly tensed under his skin. "Shhh," I whispered. "There will be no car doors to interrupt us this time."

Thomas's hands drifted along the skin on my stomach briefly, then explored excitedly between my legs, his fingers finding the wetness that had been growing since I'd spotted him watching me. We kissed, our tongues dancing alongside one another until Thomas moved his mouth to my neck, then my shoulder, tasting my skin, guzzling my excitement like water. I closed my eyes. His hard cock pushed urgently between my thighs, then against my quickly swelling clit, rocketing my need for him into overdrive.

When I opened my eyes again, I jumped slightly, startled. In the doorway stood Jacob, holding a duffle bag in one arm and a red-bowed poinsettia in another. He was staring at us, expressionless. Feeling my twitch of surprise,

Thomas pulled away and turned but did not immediately release his grip on my torso, even after he saw my fiancé at the door.

"I—I wanted to surprise you," Jacob stammered.

I did not move. Jacob didn't look angry. In fact, I thought I saw a glimmer of curiosity in his face, though he was certainly dumbfounded as well. "Jake..." I began, but I felt Thomas's arms tighten slightly around me and I stopped.

Then, it was my turn to be speechless.

Thomas silently removed one arm from my body and stretched it sideways, toward Jacob. His hand was open as if expecting Jacob to hand him something. In return, Jacob hesitated but soon dropped the bag and plant on the floor and walked slowly toward us as if in a trance. When he was within grasp, Thomas reached behind Jacob's head and pulled it gently toward his, then kissed Jacob hard on the mouth.

I watched Jacob's body relax and lean closer, and I ducked out from Thomas's other arm and positioned myself next to my fiancé. When the two men broke apart, I wordlessly pulled Jacob's clothing off, piece by piece. When he was naked, he grabbed my wrist. "You are so beautiful," he said dazedly.

I kissed him delicately on the mouth, then climbed carefully onto the bed and crawled toward the pillows, making sure to give both men an uninterrupted view of my ass.

Jacob and Thomas followed my lead, and I relaxed onto my back. I turned and pulled Jacob next to me, again kissing him softly on the lips. He positioned himself on his side, and when our mouths broke apart, I watched his eyes glide toward my chest. He reverently cupped my breast in one hand and methodically rolled his fingertip along the nipple, making my stomach quiver. Jacob leaned down and kissed my mouth, his hand stroking my thighs, then sliding softly between them.

As he began to kiss my shoulder, he rubbed himself against my hip. I looked at him, our eyes locking as he gently nudged my body to turn on my side to face Thomas. He continued to kiss my shoulder and moved downward, pressing his lips to my shoulder blade while his cock ground desperately between my cheeks.

Thomas slid down onto his side and placed his hand on the inside of my thigh, guiding it up to coax my legs open. Then the hard tip of his cock pushed against the slickness already covering my clit and slid up and back down again, sending shivers of anticipation throughout my body.

I turned my head and Jacob kissed me again, his warm chest pressing against my back. I reached back and held his face in my hand, searching his eyes with mine. "Is this okay?" I asked. I felt my heart race into my throat. Everything felt so right, so good, but reality pecked at the back of my brain.

Jacob kissed me and smiled, his eyes serious. "Yes," he whispered. "I want you so badly." He reached over me and placed his hand on Thomas, pulling him closer. "Both of you."

I squeezed Thomas's throbbing cock with my hand and guided it inside me, and Jacob began to sway back and forth, moving Thomas in and out of me. Thomas placed his hand on Jacob's ass and pushed it harder. I felt the hot tickle of orgasm begin to grow, but then Thomas withdrew. Jacob immediately took his place from behind, and Thomas bent his head down to suck at my breast as I felt my body relax into the twin sensations competing for my attention.

When Jacob pulled back, I flipped onto my back again, and Thomas immediately slid on top of me and inside me anew, this time pounding rhythmically until he was almost at climax.

As he bucked expertly between my legs, Jacob kissed him long and hard. Thomas left me and moved over to the side to guide Jacob back on top of and inside me. As Thomas climbed over to position himself on his knees in back of my fiancé, I saw Jacob's eyes widen with unbridled excitement.

Iridescent screams of orgasm washed over me like a perpetual tide, and Thomas began pushing against Jacob, forcing him deeper and deeper into me. Thomas thrusted one final time, and Jacob called out as he came, then collapsed breathlessly onto his side, his hand coming to a final rest protectively on my stomach.

Thomas rolled onto his back on the other side of me, his arms folded in a crook behind his head. After a long silence, he said, "I should probably get back to repairing the fence." Before anyone could protest, he slid sideways and over to his pile of clothing on the floor. I watched his tanned body appreciatively until the last button was fastened. He flashed me a final sly grin, then left the room, his boot steps once again echoing down the hall.

Jacob ran his hand up and down my pale torso. "You really are beautiful, my Jule," he said, his eyes on my breasts. "I couldn't ask for a better present."

I smiled. "Merry Christmas."

We never made love with the lights out again.

-END-

Ring My Bells

Honey Cummings

THURSDAY AFTERNOON

Ginger looked troubled digging through the holiday bin full of stockings, tights, and socks. Her wavy red locks were pulled back into a sloppy bun. Biting her lip, her hazel eyes bounced between the Santa Claus and Reindeer thigh high stocking sets. She shook both, but only one jingled, and she furrowed her brow. *I kind of like the idea of them jingling, but is that too much?*

"What are you doing?" Her friend marveled over the action as if it were something she'd never witnessed before.

"Tina, I can't decide if I want ones with jingle bells," she whined, looking at the collars of the reindeers where the bells hung. "I think they're cute, but I don't know."

"Well, here's some that look like an ugly Christmas sweater with poof balls." Now Tina found herself digging into the bin where a moment before she had walked past it without a second thought.

"You mean puff balls?" Ginger dropped Santa and took them from Tina, eager to weigh the new option against the doe-eyed reindeer.

"Poof, puff, smuff…" She leaned deeper into the mixture, raking huge swathes of product to the side. "Aww, they have a pair of candy cane ones with little bows."

"No, that's too common," flustered Ginger and dropped the ugly sweater pair. "No, these won't work either. They remind me of Uncle Chuck's sweaters that Aunt Jasmine would make and…" A shudder shook her. "I need something unique and borderline loud. Not something Uncle Chuck would wear," she snickered.

60

"Well, bells can be loud." Tina shook her head and pulled another pair from the depths. "I see penguins, I see snowmen…"

"No, I think I might go with these reindeer. They're the only fuzzy thigh high stockings in here that I can find, and I don't see another pair of them." She rubbed her thumbs into the material. "I think they might be the last pair, Tina."

"I call bullshit on this bin," Tina hissed, shoving her pile level again in disgust. "There's Halloween shit at the bottom. Look, bats and pumpkins. I feel cheated. There's barely any Christmas themed anything in this bin."

"I just wish they had those jumbo jingle bells on them." Ginger let the googly-eyed reindeer stockings drop into her basket next to the glow-in-the-dark condoms and bottle of Astroglide.

"They have a craft section here." Tina hooked an arm in hers and tugged Ginger deeper into the large chain store, taking stock in her basket as they went. "What kind of a holiday party are you having … and why am I not invited?"

Ginger's freckled face flushed red. "Well, Oliver is back from the UK tomorrow afternoon and won't be going anywhere … and with that blizzard coming in Friday night and hot on the heels of his flight… I uh, I thought maybe … being snowed in and all…"

Tina let out a snort-giggle, razzing her, "Girl, does Oliver have that kind of stamina to ride you for the whole blizzard?"

"Stop." She palmed Tina's face. "Just help me find bigger balls."

"Well now," Tina made a goofy expression, lowering her voice, "not sure how big Oliver's balls are, but we both know Jackson's hang—"

"Tina!" Ginger gave her a death glare.

A chill rolled through Ginger and her skin pimpled. She had casually met up with Jackson a few times, but nothing had ever come from the hook ups. Never once did he ask her out, nor did they stick around to cuddle. The one-night stand with a friends-with-benefits angle had been nice until the day she met Oliver. Both seemed to be from different worlds completely when she weighed the two men against one another.

Oliver had hit on her at a meeting between clients. Something about that suave British accent and well-dressed attire made her wet her panties when they shook hands. Such a tight grip, his hand swallowing hers, and smooth. Before they knew it, she was dropping her dress to her ankles in his hotel room and after that they started dating. A coworker had her convinced he swung the other way the last time they had met him, but at the hotel bar when his hand rode up her thigh, it was game on. With dark hair and eyes, she sold her soul to him for a chance to brag but ended up getting serious with him, even with the distance between them. The man knew how to pleasure a woman, making her beg for his cock and tease her for the long haul. The whole time they fucked it was a feral mix of moans and groans, touching soft then hard, keeping one another guessing.

His tongue, like hot silk, against her pussy had made her legs quiver. Fingers slipping into his locks of hair until she gripped a fistful. Oliver groaned as she pulled him in, hips rocking as he continued to eat her up. Another shudder rolled through her as she thought about the way he fingered her until she would start to come, only to shove his rock-hard cock into her, and make her scream and arch. Teeth on nipples, teasing and making her waver in the explosion of sensations, only to let her catch her breath, and repeat the climb again and again until she tapped out.

Yeah, Tina, Oliver does have the stamina for it...

The last time she hooked up with Jackson, he had been ravenous, pushing her over the edge and not relenting. Just hearing his name reminded her of how his body grinded deep and hard into her. With those blue eyes and dark brown hair, he towered over her. Jackson looked like a good ole boy, camouflage jacket and pants with big boots, complete with tattoos painting both arms. He worked for the tow truck company and just so happened to eat at the diner she used to be a waitress at through college. That last night, she had told him about meeting someone, and wanting to give it a real try. Even now Jackson's expression stung, leaving her chest aching.

I thought we were just fuck-buddies this whole time. He only came over to my place and was gone before morning so... why that expression?

Even now, the sensation of how he would bend her over and fuck her from behind gave her plenty to masturbate to time and time again. Sometimes he gripped her hips, and she could no longer tell if he was pulling her onto his cock or pounding and pushing into her hard as hell. Her eyes would roll back as she arched, the heat of his hand crawling across her entire body until he gripped her throat or hooked her mouth. Jackson would slow down and spank her or flip her into a new position. Never once was she allowed to pick or predict the next position. He dominated the lovemaking, and she howled with the pleasure he brought with her ankles over his shoulder. Her favorite moments were the points in which he started to peak and would at last kiss her, suckling her neck or breast at times as he came hard.

That man can release a monstrous amount of cum, so hot and...

Between the two, they were equally built. Lean and athletic, they would stand eye-to-eye next to one another. Ginger's mind continued to slip deeper into a lustful train of thought. Her imagination wandered down each of them, seeing them naked side-by-side. Tilting her head, she could easily masturbate to the thought of watching the two of them hooking up with one another. Her eyebrows lifted high, as her thoughts paused on that idea.

I'd even go as far as paying to see them make out with one another. But Jackson has the—

"I said, are these big enough?" Tina jolted her from her naughty thoughts.

"Um." Swallowing, Ginger took the giant jingle bells in hand. *These are as big as Jackson, ha!* "Yeah, these are plenty big enough."

Tina's icy fingers touched her forehead and cheek, making her wince. "You burning a fever? Your face is all flushed and red."

Ginger shoved her off and laughed. "Not the kind I need a doctor for."

"Oh, not the kind you need an MD for," Tina nudged her with an elbow, "but the kind that comes with a dose of the D, eh?"

"Where do you come up with these ridiculous innuendos?" marveled Ginger.

"Oh, come on now." Tina motioned to the store, giggling. "You can make anything into a sexual innuendo. Especially in the produce section where everything can look phallic as fuck."

Ginger realized an old woman pushing her buggy had overheard them and her expression softened. "Ain't that the truth, honey!" the old woman cackled pushing past them. "Y'all remind me of myself when I was that age! I'm too old to rock my hips like that, so enjoy it while you can, sweetie."

Ginger's face turned bright red as she covered it, glaring at Tina through her fingers.

"Remind me that I talk too damn loud for these sorts of conversations in public places," mumbled Tina.

FRIDAY AFTERNOON

Ginger had laid out the reindeer stockings adorning their new giant bells (courtesy of Tina's impromptu sewing skills). Fresh from the shower, she let the towel drop to the floor as she dug through the closet. *What should I wear with these fuzzy stockings?* Pulling out a cute sundress, she shook her head and shoved it back. *It's getting cold tonight and that's more spring or summertime.* Another pull and she had the sexy red dress she wore to last year's holiday party. *Oliver did see me in this one.* Holding it up to the googly eyes of the reindeers, she cringed. *Oh, that's a terrible match up.* Reaching into the closet once more, she passed outfit after outfit until her hand grazed a soft sweater. *Alpaca sweater. So soft...* She paused and pulled out the pink sweater, a gift from Jackson she hadn't worn because it was too large and bulky to wear over an outfit without swamping her, but a thought crossed her mind. *Stockings, sweater, and maybe some lacy panties?*

Pulling the sweater on, she pulled it down, and walked over to her mirror. *Sans-panties... this covers just enough, like a pajama shirt.* The sleeves covered down to her knuckles minus her fingers and the bottom hem was close to midthigh. *Crap, is this too long to wear with the stockings?* Pulling on the stockings, she loved the silken fleece against her freshly shaved legs. The bells jangled the whole way onto her legs and she laughed. *How fun!* Jumping to her feet, she jingled with each step back to the mirror and snorted at herself. *This is exactly what I wanted!*

Standing before the mirror, her eyes lit up. *This is it. This is the cute effect I wanted to have.* The fuzzy sweater and turtleneck helped complete her look that screamed adorable and cozy. *I'll leave my hair in a bun. It looks fine.* The material snug, despite being oversized, added to her curves, and did nothing to hide her breasts and nipples. *Yeah, I look ready to fuck in this!*

Grabbing her cell phone from the bed, she saw it was almost time for Oliver to arrive at any point. Jingling her way to the kitchen, she poured a glass of wine and sat in her warm living room where the fireplace crackled. *And now we wait.*

About three glasses in, her heart began to ache. *He should have been in thirty minutes ago.* Inhaling deep, she hadn't thought to ask for which flight he was coming in on. *What if it was canceled? No, he would have called me then. Maybe delayed? Rerouted?* She pulled up the weather report and sighed. *Seems like it's moving in faster than they thought.* As if the forces heard her thoughts, Oliver's text popped up.

[Oliver: Flight just landed. Bumpy but they said it may take a while to get luggage unloaded. Miss you! Can't wait to see you!]

[Ginger: I was starting to worry! Stay safe and I'm here waiting with a warm fire! XOXO]

[Oliver: Sounds divine, my love! ;)]

Flopping her head back, she scoffed. *Now what do I do? I'm all worked up and he might not be coming through the door for an hour or more. It's like a for-ty-minute drive without a blizzard moving in. Ugh!*

Swishing her last sip of wine, she gulped it down. *Damn. More wine is in order.* Marching back to the kitchen, she poured more. Pausing on a sip, she grinned to herself. *I was gonna save the outfit for when he got here, but maybe I can send him some naughty pictures.* Wiggling onto the couch, she flustered over the idea of having to wait. Feet pointed at the ceiling, the fire and tree behind, the googly-eyed reindeer looked just as sad as she was over the delay. She snapped a few shots, and then nodded once she got a clear shot, the background blurred just slightly. *Damn, my legs look sexy in these stockings!*

Laying back on the couch, she sat in the silence of her home snapping photos. She made a pouty face, the image capturing the obvious fact she was completely nude and braless under the fuzzy sweater. The pink really made her face look worthy of a blushing bride. *Yeah! That's the stuff.* Outside, the sound of snow tip-tapping on the roof and ground, a harsh murmuring to the snap and crackle. Her fingers fidgeted with the hem of the sweater, and she bit her lip. *Well, if it's going to be a while...*

Launching off the couch, she gulped down the glass of wine and the three sips left in the bottle. *I'll pop the other bottle when Oliver arrives. Now, to the bedroom for some sultry boudoir pictures.* Armed with her cell phone and feeling the liquid courage fueling her dirty desires, she stood in front of the mirror posing in all sorts of ways. Sometimes she would lift the hem just enough for her ass cheeks to peek, or her shaven pussy, while others she pulled on the sweater this way and that. At last, she sat on her bed sending the images.

[Oliver: You tease!]

[Ginger: It's killing me to wait too!]

[Oliver: Keep sending me pics, my love! Please!]

Biting her lip, she couldn't fight how horny and flustered she felt.

[Ginger: Send me a pic first.]

[Oliver: Well, I have time...]

Ginger sat up in alarm, eyes wide as she gasped. *Is he really going to send me a pic from the airport? He wouldn't...* She jumped to her feet, a flurry of jingling as she paced back and forth waiting for the next text.

[Oliver: You've already got me so hard right now. *dick pic*]

Squealing, Ginger licked her lips seeing his cock on her phone.

[Oliver: You need more?]

[Oliver: *Video of him rubbing his cock: "You got me so hard, my love. Show me some more..." gruffed Oliver in his British accent.*]

[Oliver: Your turn now ;)]

"Ah! That's hot. I need to save these for material later." Ginger stole a glance at herself in the mirror. "Shit, how do I want to do this... maybe use the mirror and..." Looking around her room, she grabbed the sitting chair from the corner, dragging it to the mirror. "Wait, better lighting..." Rushing to her bathroom, she brought over her makeup light and mirror and plugged it in. "Ha! And with the clamp I can get picture worthy lighting on my va-jay-jay!"

Ginger sat in the chair and wiggled one way and then the other to find a cute pose to send and hint what the next few shots would provide. Pulling the sweater up, she parted her legs and took a shot of her pussy and another with her fingers playing with her clit.

[Oliver: Yes! Oh yes, I'm so hard! *dick pic with pre-cum*]

She struggled to take the next shot she wanted: a clear view of her fingering herself.

[Oliver: Don't stop]

"Trying not to!" she fussed, hating the last barrage of photos.

[Oliver: I want a video and I'll send one of me cumming for you]

"Oh!" she stared at the promise and smirked. "I want a video of that!"

Again, she fumbled with the phone to video it. *Fuck, I'm too drunk to coordinate this.* Looking to the light, an idea struck her. *Time to clamp the phone and straddle the camera, ha!*

[Oliver: Please baby, show me more]

"Working on it! So impatient!"

[Oliver: So close, so close and wanting to see your pussy one more time]

Ginger finally started getting better pictures. Slumping into the chair so she could capture herself groping a breast in the background or her biting her lips, she sent shot after shot.

[Oliver: *video of him cumming: "I can't wait to unload on you and fuck you in that pretty pink sweater, my love."*]

Wanting to match Oliver's own video, she managed to capture herself playing with her clit until she came. Her pussy dripping wet caught vividly thanks to the impromptu lighting. Reaching over, she grabbed her phone, panting, and tried sending it.

[Ginger: *video* *Unable to send*]

"Bullshit," she muttered, belly flopping on her bed she fought to send it. *What if I send from the video itself?* She went through the gallery, hit the share button, went to press the icon for Oliver and as her thumb hit it, the option refreshed to someone else and went away.

"What the fuck?"

Panicking, she flipped back into the messages side to see where her pussy went and dread filled her.

[Jackson: So, is it safe to assume you sent that by mistake since you said Oliver and not my name?]

Covering her face, she stared at the text. "Oh no."

[Ginger: Sorry, I'm drunk and don't know how my phone works.]

Burying her face into her pillow she screamed. "I'm a moron! Never sexting again!"

Friday Night

Ginger jolted awake, her buzz long gone and the fire low as the house sat dark. Another round of knocking at her door made her rush to the living room. *Oliver!* Outside, the wind howled. It was late, far later. Her phone was filled with missed calls and texts. *I passed out hard. Crap!* Swinging the door open, she flinched as a wall of icy wind slammed her. When she finally looked back, the build and face that greeted her was—

"Jackson?" Ginger tugged the sweater down. *Fuck! And I'm still naked under this!*

"Huh?" Jackson's eyes dipped and he snorted. "Always thought it would look cute on you. Glad to see you wear only it."

Her face reddened, biting her lips as her panicked thoughts clashed into one another. *What do I say? Why is he here? He bought this for me last Christmas and—*

"My love!" Oliver's voice brought her behind Jackson where the British Adonis leaned into view. "Did you fall asleep waiting on me?" he chortled, pushing past Jackson to scoop her up.

Ginger squealed, "You're so cold! What took so long?"

"The bridge is bad getting into this side of town, and he was lucky to make it across at all." Jackson closed the door, inviting himself in and squatting in front of the burning coals.

"Yes, Jackson told me on the way here you two knew each other *very well*." Oliver kissed Ginger before starting to shed his overcoat. "How lucky I was to have him give me a tow."

"Um, we do … know each other." Ginger watched as Jackson began to get the fire up and going again, warming his hands by it. "It's been a while…"

Jackson looked over his shoulder, his eyes looking at her legs. "Cute socks. That new?"

"Y-yeah…" Ginger shook her head, pulling the hem of the sweater down as Oliver hung up his coat. "Thank you for getting the fire going and … helping Oliver make it here."

"Well, weather was giving us hell to get here, so I'm stuck." Jackson stood, furrowing his brow at her outfit. "Sorry to … interrupt your night."

"Nonsense," interjected Oliver, helping Jackson pull off his coat. "Let me help you take this off; make yourself at home."

"Don't mind if I do." Jackson smirked and winked at Ginger.

Scowling, she watched in horror as Oliver hung up Jackson's coat. "I guess you can stay for a little while." Unhappy, she marched into the kitchen and popped open her second bottle of wine. "Don't mind me."

Oliver had huddled in front of the fire with Jackson, the two whispering back and forth. *Ugh, look at Jackson getting chummy with Oliver. Such a cock block.* Jackson's eyebrows lifted high in response to something Oliver said, and they both shot a look back at her. She gave her fakest smile and started gulping the wine in her glass. *Don't fucking look at me! I'm here minding my own business, horny and... ugh!* Refilling the glass, she glared at them as Oliver slid closer to Jackson, throwing an arm around him and obscuring their lips. *I can't read lips, but I still feel angry at losing all chances to figure out what they are talking about.* She began to sip her wine watching Oliver's hand slide down Jackson's hard-muscled back and grope his ass—

Coughing and sputtering, she wheezed.

"You okay, baby?" Oliver was in the kitchen in a flash.

Unable to say anything as she recovered, she shot a look at Jackson who stayed huddled at the fire unphased. *Was that my imagination or did Oliver just goose my Ex-Fuck-Buddy's ass?*

"I'm sorry, love." Oliver spun her around, moving the bottle and glass to the side to pick her up to sit on the counter. "I guess I left something turned on in the kitchen, huh?"

"Yes..." She took one inhale, relieved to have found her voice again.

"How about I do something about that?" he whispered, icy fingers slipping between her thighs.

Whimpering, she whispered, "Your fingers are fucking cold."

"I know, but there's a warm place right here," Oliver cooed.

Ginger's breath caught as fingers rubbed across her pussy, slick with her arousal. She parted her legs, the reindeer jingling softly. Fingers dipped inside her, and she stifled the moan she so desperately wanted to make. *But Jackson is just there in the living room! This is so...* Oliver's fingers slid up and began circling her clit. Ginger closed her eyes tight. *I'll lose my bravery if I see Jackson, not opening my eyes until we're done!* His lips pressed hard against hers and she deepened the kiss. *That's right, as far as he knows we're making out. Ha! Take that Mr. Cock-Block!* She rose her knees, another flutter of jingles, as she moaned into his mouth. Oliver suckled on her tongue, his fingers dipped back into her pussy, and she hugged his neck. His other hand groped her breast through the fuzzy material, her nipples growing more sensitive as her pleasure climbed.

The sound of Oliver's pants unbuckling made her pussy tighten on his thrusting fingers. Ginger's brow furrowed. *Wait a minute here...* Fingers rolled up, playing with her clit again disrupted her thoughts. She could hear his pants hit the floor as the tip of his hard cock teased her opening while another arm jerked—*Another arm?* Oliver moaned into her mouth and pinched her nipple. Another hand sent the reindeers into alarm mode as it lifted her one ankle onto Oliver's shoulder. Her eyes flew open, Jackson right behind Oliver.

Breaking the kiss with Oliver, she took it all in as Jackson stroked Oliver's cock while Oliver's hands were full with her. *But where is...* Jackson's pants were open and his own erection not in view as he—*pressed it against Oliver's ass cheeks?!*

"What the hell is going on?" Ginger's voice was high-pitched.

"A threesome?" offered Jackson.

Oliver leaned in and whispered, "Please baby, he's so fucking hot and when I saw you sent him the video meant for me, I couldn't resist offering."

"A threesome." Ginger paled. *Dammit, Tina! It's a trap! I'm the one with the questionable stamina!* "I, I don't think I can keep up with both?" *AH! Why did I say that?*

Oliver chuckled and leaned into Jackson, "That's okay. We can play with each other while you rest, my love."

Ginger could see the imaginary nosebleed erupting from her nostrils at this point. Jackson with his epic five o'clock shadow, broad shoulders, and lumberjack arms stroking the cock of her dark-eyed, clean-cut British Adonis. *Play with each other?* The two started to kiss, Jackson stroking and grinding behind Oliver. *Did I slip and hit my head at the department store?* Pulling away, Oliver knelt before Jackson's rock-hard dick and began licking it. Ginger arched a brow, watching as he took in Jackson's monster cock, but Jackson's eyes were on her.

Biting her lip, she wiggled on the counter to get into a more provocative position. Her hands slid down between her open legs as she began to play with herself. Jackson moaned as Oliver's hand snaked up and under his shirt. He licked his lips before bending down. Her hands retreated in time to feel the heat of his silken tongue across her pussy. A whimper escaped her, bells jingling as her legs shook. Jackson suckled and ate her out while Oliver pushed and pulled his dick in and out of those fleshy lips.

"Shit," she rasped. "I'm cumming..." As if some secret password had been spoken, the men stopped their festivities "What's wrong?"

"You get the first pop," Jackson offered Oliver.

"Such as gentlemen." Oliver leaned into Jackson, their cocks touching as he retrieved something from a bag. "But you can have the pleasure of popping us both off." He handed Jackson the bottle of Astroglide and condoms.

Oh shit! I did leave the bag there! I don't know what's about to happen, but something tells me I'm gonna be cumming too hard to care!

Midnight Bells

Wicked grins crossed the men's faces. Condoms and lube in place, they at last turned their attention back to Ginger. She gasped. *I mean, it's a tad much. I've slept with both of them, just never at the same time. One can lick*—Oliver's tongue dipped between the folds of her pussy and a leg bucked, bells ringing. As he suckled and slurped, Jackson was quick to raise her ankle to his shoulders. Jackson's eyes on her, he pushed forward with a grunt, and Oliver moaned into her, making her legs shake, more bells jingling.

"Fucking ring my bells!" She gripped the counter edge, white-knuckled. *Can someone pass out from too much pleasure? Shit, I'm about to find out!*

Oliver's hands glided over her hips, pushing the sweater up until her breasts were exposed. Humming, he kissed his way up her body, her skin pimpling. As Oliver's lip encapsulated a nipple, she could feel Jackson guide Oliver's cock into her pussy. *So, fucking hot. Jackson is never so gentle*—Jackson pushed hard with his hip into Oliver, who in turn thrusted forward into her, and she yelped with pleasure. *He's going to fuck me using Oliver–MY HEART!* Oliver sucked hard on her nipple, moaning. Jackson's hand slid between where she and Oliver connected, and her pussy tightened.

Through heavy eyelids, she met Jackson's gaze. He bit his lip, something he only did when he was enjoying himself. As his fingers rubbed Oliver's cock, he pulled Oliver back and pushed forward. Ginger dripped, hot and wet, swollen with the arousal swallowing her. She arched into them, both lovers finding a way to fuck her at the same time. The bells rang in a steady and hypnotic sound, like the bells on a clock striking midnight. Jackson's hand shifted between them, and a thumb began to circle her clit.

A hard ring of bells signaled her climax. Jackson retreated his hand. Oliver pounded hard and fast into her by proxy of Jackson. The familiar rhythm rocking both her and Oliver. Her orgasm, unrelenting, as she howled in pleasure. Oliver's lips pressed against hers, moaning into one another's mouths as Jackson drove him into her. The motion stopped; Jackson pulled away.

"Fucking clothes," he grumbled, kicking off boots, and shedding everything.

Oliver laughed, his forehead meeting hers as they caught their breath. "Did you really give this amazing man up for me?"

She tensed and his cock throbbed in reply. "Well, we weren't dating?" *Shit, Jackson heard me.*

Jackson's intense expression softened. "I told Oliver he took away my best fuck-buddy and if he ever wanted to tag-team, let me know. Granted, I was joking…"

"Was," cooed Oliver, pulling away from her to strip down too. "So, I made an offer."

"Yeah, cute pics you sent him. Not going to lie—you never sexted with me." Jackson pulled the condom off and tossed it in the trashcan.

"But I was miffed to find out you accidentally sent him the video," Oliver also discarded his own condom, "and didn't even send it to me."

"S-sorry. I had a bottle of wine and after was screaming into my pillow with embarrassment." Ginger shifted and winced, changing the subject, "Uh, my ass hurts on this granite countertop, so can we move to the bed? Pretty please?" she asked, unsure if her two hunks would agree.

"Only if you lose the sweater," offered Jackson with an arched brow.

"But keep those stockings. I rather enjoy hearing them ring," added Oliver.

Excited and nervous, Ginger's steps jangled with anticipation. The boys scooped up the condoms and Astroglide as they led the way. Her heartbeat thudded hard against her chest. *This is really happening. I'm in a threesome with the two best lovers I've ever had in my life.* Oliver sat on her bed, rolling on a fresh condom on and making it slick with lube. Jackson snuck behind her, wrapping her with his monstrous arms from behind to fondle her, teasing her pussy and pinching a nipple as she squirmed.

"You ready for what we have planned next, my little fuck-bunny?" the heat of his breath over her neck and shoulder added to the chills rolling through her.

"A-and … w-what is that?" Ginger stuttered, the erotic petting making it hard to form thoughts, let alone words.

"You still like anal? Right?" he gruffed, a hand sliding slowly across her hip and across her ass. "Hmm?"

"Y-yes," she confessed as he slid a lubed finger inside her ass.

A moan escaped her as he stretched and stroked her, all while marching her toward Oliver. Her knees shook, and he spun her and grinned. Oliver's knees slipped between her own and she sat, the tip of his cock knocking at her backdoor. Her heart fluttered as she eased down onto him until his dick's full length was inside. Jackson laid her down on top of Oliver whose hands glided hot over her body to grope both breasts as he suckled at her neck. Jackson knelt and began licking and suckling at her clit, she barely noticed the hand taking a condom and lube to do his own preparations.

Oliver began to grind in and out of her, and before she could fully react, Jackson's monster cock was slipping inside her pussy. Her body arched, two hard dicks filling her as Jackson's grip held her hips in place. Panting, she stared up at Jackson bewildered, the sensation so pleasurable, that every little movement threatened to tip her into another orgasm. Jackson peered down at them, his eyes dancing between her and Oliver.

Oliver's voice cooed over her shoulder, "What are you waiting for, Big Boy?"

Jackson smirked, scoffing, "Just wondering which of you cupcakes are going to come first."

Ginger shuddered as Jackson began to slowly grind, the muscles in his abdomen rolled from between her legs. Oliver began to match pace, the two hard cocks rubbing so many places all at once. *This is pure bliss!* Her body shook, the orgasm exploding, as her moaning turned to screaming. Jackson picked up pace, she could feel herself coming hard, again and squirting. The hot liquid trickled down, and Oliver moaned, starting to fuck her ass faster to keep up with Jackson.

If I'm going to faint from too much sexual pleasure this should be the—

Another climax waved through her, and she arched. Oliver's body tensed and he pressed hard into her, his cock hard as he came. Jackson leaned on top of them, dominating them both as he grunted with each hard and fast pound of his cock. Now, he had them both wailing in ecstasy, his hard dick keeping her coming and rubbing against Oliver's own cock still throbbing inside her. The ringing of the bells barely audible through her moaning and pleasurable shrieks with each pound. *I'm not going to be able to sit or walk without feeling sensitive and wanting more! These boys have spoiled me!*

Oliver was starting to join in again. *How long has Jackson been going? He's never lasted this long! He's giving this his-all in case this is the last time—*

Sweat dripped from Jackson's body, her skin pimpling and the sensation animalistic. Another orgasm and he grunted, his cock throbbing. Oliver was growing hard again, the out of sync fucking making her breath catch. *I can't moan or scream anymore! This is unearthly!* Jackson was so close, and he stopped thrusting... *He lost it again.* He slowed, panting as he gave them a desperate expression.

"I can't cum." Jackson swallowed, trying to slow his beating heart.

"Is it the bells?" asked Ginger.

Jackson shook his head, trying to catch his breath.

"Is it me?" Oliver offered.

"No." Jackson furrowed his brow and pulled away so they could sit up.

He was pacing the floor, looking like he just ran a marathon when Ginger asked, "Then what's wrong?"

Jackson pointed at the socks, pulling the condom off in frustration. "It's impossible to cum when a pair of googly-eyed reindeer are grinning up at me the whole time!"

Ginger lost it. Laughter rolling from her. "OH MY—"

"Poor man." Oliver chortled before concluding, "Ginger, go lose the socks and hop in the shower, my love. You're all wet, and I'm about to blow this monster cock."

"I'm not missing this!" guffawed Ginger.

Oliver knelt before Jackson who seemed a little bashful. "First time letting a man suck your cock?"

Jackson blew out his cheeks and covered his mouth, confessing, "Y-yeah."

Oliver took his length hard and deep into him and Jackson moaned. Slipping the socks off, she kicked them under her bed and out of sight. Jackson locked eyes with her, eating up her flushed body on the bed. She opened her legs, showing him her world as he grabbed Oliver's head and began grinding into the heat of his mouth. Another moan escaped him as Oliver deep throated his cock. Ginger's hands slipped between her thighs, watching Oliver choke down Jackson's cock. Another moan and she gasped, touching her swollen pussy. Jackson grunted, pressed hard into Oliver, *and he swallowed! I don't even swallow!*

The two men stumbled back to the bed, belly flopping on either side of her. *Best blizzard snowed-in slumber party ever. Should have invited Tina. Fuck!*

The Holiday Switch

Ali Whippe

7:30PM

The annual Holiday Bash at the Honey Pot is always a sold-out event. From vendors who want to cut loose and join the fun to employees who want the chance to relax and explore their fantasies, the tickets are always a prized commodity–and the twist that the regular clubbers might get chosen to serve as the employees for the first part of the night is a huge draw for those who don't normally lean toward submission but are willing to try it out for an evening's pleasure.

"Who are you looking for tonight?" Samantha asks, the manager turning to the bartender with a raised eyebrow. "I want Suzy to be me tonight. I want to watch her watch everyone else having fun and not be able to join in anything until midnight." She tosses her dark hair over her shoulder. "The woman needs to learn patience."

Zoey giggles, the tiny bartender moving closer so she can whisper into her friend's ear. "Oh, definitely Carter. I want to watch that huge man struggle behind the bar ... in a thong."

"Or nothing at all!" Samantha agrees, picturing the big man's muscular back and thighs.

"Wait," Zoey says, eye alight with an idea. "What if we make him work the whole night ... with his clothes on?" Samantha bursts out laughing, both of them knowing that Carter is naked almost immediately after he walks in the door, eager to share his monstrous cock and superb skills with everyone. Zoey grins, scanning the employee room for Kylie, the tall blonde who normally manages

74

the cages. Catching her eye, she waves her over, taking in the sexy red velvet corset, garter belt, and white thigh high stockings. Kylie is already dressed for the party, steady in her five-inch heels as she is in her normal skimpy black dress and spiked leather boots on an ordinary night at the club. Her blonde hair is tied up into two buns on top of her head, and she looks adorable—a very different vibe from the dominatrix she normally is.

"What's up, ladies?" Kylie asks, joining them. Samantha tugs her shirt over her head, revealing her large breasts as she nods her head at Zoey. She pulls a lacy bra from her bag, wrapping it around her back and clasping the front as Kylie turns her attention to the bartender. "You have a naughty idea," she guesses. "Spill it."

"You know Carter, right?"

Kylie sighs. "Who doesn't know Carter? That man is beautiful ... and knows it."

"Exactly," Zoey says. "I'm going to pick him tonight if I can."

Kylie snorts. "Shove that man behind the bar? Girl, you are devilish!"

"Wait, it gets better," Samantha adds, leaning in as she drags stockings up one leg. "Tell her the rest."

"I'm going to make him work behind the bar all night ... with his clothes on."

Kylie stares at her for a moment, the idea sinking in, and then she laughs hard, a glint of the mistress peeking out even though she isn't working tonight. "That is diabolical," she says, giving Zoey an appraising look. "You sure you don't want to move over to my area? Your talents are wasted behind that bar."

Samantha reaches out and puts an arm around Zoey's shoulders, tugging the smaller girl close. "Hey, no poaching!" she orders. "Zoey's the best bartender I've had in years. Her talent is perfectly used every night."

Kylie gives Zoey a long look, then sniffs and rolls her eyes. "Suit yourself," the dominatrix says. "Tonight, I'm picking Luca."

Both women squeal in delight. "Luca! But he hates telling people what to do!" Zoey says.

"And even when he does ask for something, he's always super polite about it," Samantha adds. "You're going to make that poor man order everyone about?"

"Oh yeah," Kylie says with a wink. "It's going to be awesome."

Samantha finishes getting dressed, then glances at Zoey, who still wears cut-off jean shorts and a white tank top. "You getting changed?"

Zoey shakes her head. "Hell no. I always get gussied up and wear my sexi-ness–since some of us have to earn tips in other ways," she says with a glance at Kylie. "Tonight, I'm going to be comfortable."

"You go, girl," Samantha says and Kylie nods in approval. The trio glance at the door at the sound of more employees entering. Two large men enter together, the bouncers' faces relaxed and welcoming instead of the reserved distance they normally adopt. Will wears blue jeans and a black t-shirt, a casual look compared to Tom, who still sports the formal dark suit he normally wears at work. "You boys looking forward to tonight?"

"Men," Tom says, giving Samantha's lingerie an appreciative look. "Don't sexually harass us with demeaning names."

Will gives him a push on the arm, winking at Zoey. "Dude, the whole point of tonight is to sexually harass everyone here. For once, we get to actually join in instead of watching and hauling out creeps."

Tom rolls his eyes at that. Though there has been the occasional creep at an event, most of the time, the clientele at the club are great—fun to watch and better to listen to. There's a reason they only need two bouncers for the whole place. People come here for a consenting good time, and they leave satisfied.

"Looking good, Boss Lady," Will comments, then turns his attention to Kylie and Zoey. "Lovely as always," he says, then adds, "Different for sure, and it's very nice."

"Thanks," Samantha replies, eyeing Will's broad shoulders in the t-shirt. "You too, sir."

"So," Zoey leans in close, "who are you thinking for tonight?"

Tom gives Samantha a hot look, eyes filled with promise, then glances at Will. "That's easy—the twins."

"Which ones?" Kylie asks. "The Farrah sisters or the Tackon brothers?" Everyone knows who she is talking about. The Farrah sisters are tiny dark-haired pixies and the Tackon twins are tall and lean athletes who enjoy holding partners in the air while they have sex.

"Serena and Selina," Tom answers. "They're so used to spending the night being tossed around—we want them to stand around and watch tonight. And if someone does get feisty, I want to watch them haul them outside."

Everyone laughs at the prospect of the tiny pixies hauling anyone around. "More like they'd subdue the jerk with their feminine wiles," Samantha says.

Zoey nods. "That's true. They just have to start kissing and anyone will stop being an idiot to drool." She looks around the group. "Did you see them at the Halloween party? Both twins spent the night sharing couples on the big platform. It was like watching naked Cirque du Soleil."

Will nods, biting his lip as he scans Zoey's plain clothing, the bouncer clearly making plans.

"So, what about the Tackons then?" Zoey asks, enjoying the attention. "Who do you think will grab them?" They scan the rest of the room seeing a handful of other employees—the cocktail staff are hovered in a small cluster with the few people from the kitchen staff. The Honey Pot doesn't serve food, but they provide drinks all night long, both from the bar and delivered to thirsty customers, so they have a small wait staff—three servers and two backroom busboys and dishwashers. All five of them are out of the usual black uniform tonight, their specialized trays resting on the table nearby, whispering among themselves, no doubt claiming patrons. There will still be more customers than staff tonight, but for the few who are chosen to participate in the switch, it's a chance for something different.

Samantha glances at the clock on the back wall, then stands up, clapping her hands to get everyone's attention. "Customers arriving in 15, people," she says. "Let's get the raffle set up." She scans the employees, searching for Jessica, her assistant and the organizer of tonight's events. "Jess, make sure everyone gets a number." The redhead scurries around the room, holding a hat with a bunch of folded paper inside. Each employee reaches inside and selects a paper, then heads out to the main room. When only Samantha and Jessica remain in the room, the manager reminds her assistant, "Don't forget Jenna downstairs at the front door."

Jessica flashes her a grin. "Already got her," she says. "She got first pick."

"And you?" Samantha presses. "Did you take a number?"

Jessica reaches into the hat to pluck the last folded scrap, then sets the bucket hat atop her head. She holds out her arm to Samantha, as if to escort her into the front room, which they can hear is buzzing with activity. "Shall we?"

Samantha accepts the arm, and the two make their way into the party.

8:00PM

The main room is set up in the normal party configuration: three cages—two along the side walls and one near the bar along the back wall—and two St. Andrews' crosses—one upright and one horizontal so patrons can stand or lay as they choose; three benches of various widths spread between two larger bed-sized padded furniture suited for many bodies; two padded squares on the floor with hooks for securing cuffs or bonds; a spanking horse near a spanking stand; a sex swing in one corner; several wide chairs and couches; and a traditional pole with dangling cuffs.

None of the patrons have started playing yet, all fifty attendees milling about, commenting on the outfits, the holidays, the lottery tonight, though Kylie can see Carter eyeing his favorite bench and flashing his charming smile already. She smiles, hoping that Zoey's number is low, and she gets to pick early.

Samantha and Jessica enter, and there is a small round of applause to the women who make the club a success the rest of the year.

"Thank you all for coming to the Honey Pot Annual Holiday Bash!" Samantha greets, and there are random cheers and woots. "Now, before we begin the festivities, I see that some of you are new this year, so let's review the rules. Tonight is all about employee appreciation–rewarding the people who serve you–or let you serve them–the rest of the year." She glances at Kylie, who gives a graceful bow to the audience, some of whom whistle at her, shouting, "Thank you, Mistress!"

"Tonight, our employees will enjoy a well-deserved break–and they get to choose their temporary replacements." She looks around, making sure that all eleven Honey Pot workers are present. Seeing that Jenna has arrived, standing by the closed door in front of Will and Tom, she nods. "We've already drawn numbers, so as each number is called, that employee will get to select their replacement. As the highest number, twelve will get to choose anyone–even if they have already been selected–and that person will have to choose another." Samantha looks over the crowd, then finds each of her employees. "Any questions?"

"Does this mean we finally get to play with you tonight?" A voice calls out, and Samantha laughs.

"Maybe!" she assures the speaker, a tall man with a shaved head. "Now, let's begin." She looks around. "Who has number one?"

Kylie holds up a small piece of paper. "I do!" she says, then walks over to hand it to Samantha. She turns to the crowd, many of them eagerly hoping to be chosen. Kylie takes her time, scanning the patrons before her eyes lock on the one she wants. "Come here, Luca," she says, crooking her finger at the slim Frenchman. "Tonight, you are a dom."

Luca leans down to kiss the blonde at his side, then makes his way through the crowd like a man heading to his execution. Though he plays the part of reluctant winner well, Kylie can sense something beneath, a quiet urge being satisfied as she takes his hand and leads him to stand near the employee doorway, waiting for the rest of the staff to make their selections.

"And number two?" Samantha prompts.

One of the servers raises her hand, bouncing forward to show her paper before locking eyes with a tiny blonde woman in the audience. "Serena," she says, gesturing to one of the Farrah twins, "get over here, sweetness. Tonight you're a server!"

The twin gives her sister a longing look, then heads through the crowd to stand next to the server. Samantha glances over at Tom and Will, who have huddled into a quiet conversation, no doubt making a new plan.

"Who has three?" Samantha resumes.

Tom raises his hand, then steps forward, his suit accentuating his broad shoulders. He purses his lips, skimming the crowd, then his gaze settles on a tall athletic man near the back standing next to his identical twin. "Dmitri," he says, "come on up." The Tackon twin makes his way to the front. "You're a bouncer tonight, my man!"

Samantha laughs at the look on Dmitri's face as he narrows his eyes at his twin, Darius, who has moved next to a tall blonde in a red dress, no doubt choosing his first companion for the evening.

"And number four?"

The busboy, a young man, raises his hand, then walks slowly to the front of the room. He is clearly shy in front of the crowd but still eager to choose his replacement. He shows Samantha his paper, then steps over to whisper in the ear of a young woman standing near the edge of the crowd. She wears a simple black dress and black boots, and she nods at whatever he says, following him over to the growing crowd of people near the employee room.

Numbers five, six, and seven are the remaining servers and dishwasher, who each select their patron. One server chooses a big breasted woman with short dark hair and the other picks a large man wearing nipple rings and leather briefs. Samantha knows which tray he will be carrying tonight–the one with the chain designed to slip through those rings and keep tension as he carries the serving tray. The dishwasher, an older woman who always wears her hair in a bun, chooses a man wearing jeans and a t-shirt, laughing joyfully as he says something to her.

"Eight?" Samantha resumes.

"That's me!" Zoey bounds over to show her number, then walks through the crowd to grab Carter's hand and drag him away from the crowd of adoring men and women he has already started to gather. "Not tonight, buddy," she tells the huge man. "This time, you get to watch us have all the fun while you sling drinks behind the bar."

"Only if you promise to show me how to make the drinks," he says.

"You know how to make the drinks," she tells him, "and maybe if you're very good, I'll let you lick one from between my thighs later tonight."

"Yes, ma'am," Carter agrees, following Zoey to join the crowd of employees. "Nine?"

Will raises his hand, looking over one more time at Tom who is leaning down to say something to Dmitri. He shows his number to the manager, then scans the crowd, finally settling on a tiny pixie who normally arrives with Carter. "Come on, sweetheart," he says, gesturing for her to come forward, "let me show you how to bounce."

"I know how to bounce," she says sweetly. "Maybe later I'll bounce on your cock."

"Definitely," Will laughs, walking over to join his fellow employees.

"Ten is me," Samantha announces, scanning the crowd until she locks eyes with Suzy, the buxom flirt breaking into a broad grin as she steps up. "And tonight, Suzy is managing things!"

"Awesome!" Suzy says. "I love being in charge!"

"Yep, it's great," Samantha says, "you have to make sure everything runs smoothly for the next few hours." She pauses long enough for Suzy to get really excited, then adds, "That means no sex for you." Suzy's face falls, and she frowns.

"No sex?" she exclaims. "No!"

"Not until midnight when we switch back," Samantha tells her. "Now go wait over there, and I'll give you the rundown when we're done here." Suzy makes a face but obeys and joins the others.

Samantha looks around. "Who's left?" she asks. "Eleven?"

Her assistant Jessica raises her hand, then scans the crowd, pointing at Emily and Ryan, a couple who occasionally visit the club. Her finger swings back and forth between them, then settles on Ryan, who blows his wife a kiss before heading Jessica's direction.

"And finally, twelve?" Samantha asks.

Jenna, the girl who works the front table, timidly raises her hand. She shows her paper to the manager, then looks around the room.

"Now you're last," Samantha reminds her, "so you can pick anyone here—even if they've already been picked."

Jenna considers the crowd near the employee door, then moves her attention to the remaining patrons. She settles on a small young man hovering near the door, smiling shyly as she gestures him forward. "Steven," she says softly. "You can be with me tonight." She pauses, face reddening, still shy despite her job. "I mean, you can be me tonight."

Steven smiles, biting his lip as he gives Jenna a hot look, then follows her to the crowd.

"Now," Samantha announces, "we need to give our replacements their orders for the evening, so please find a way to entertain yourselves for the next few minutes until we can get everyone setup. Happy holidays from the Honey Pot!"

The crowd cheers, some people leaning down or over to begin kissing their newfound partners while others begin drifting to various pieces of furniture.

Samantha makes her way to the employee room, leading everyone inside before finding Suzy. "Now," she begins, "here's what you need to do…"

8:30PM

Jenna leads Steven through the closed door and down the stairs to the small table and stool at the bottom. She steps behind the table, her normal spot for checking IDs and tickets for entrance. The entrance to the Honey Pot is near another club, so she occasionally has to explain to lost customers that upstairs is a private party not open to the public.

"You shouldn't have too many people coming now," Jenna explains to Steven, the young man crowding into the space with her. She retrieves the small lockbox from beneath the table, then opens the combination to pull out a ticket. "This is what the tickets for tonight look like. They all have this number and letter combination here," she points at it, "so if you see one that is all letters or numbers, it's fake." She pulls out the stack of redeemed tickets, showing him the sequential tickets. "They're all numbered, so you can tell that way, too."

"So, you just sit down here the whole night," Steven says, eyes drifting back up the staircase, "while up there, we get to…" His voice drifts off, and he looks at her, one eyebrow raised. "Are you just not into that scene?"

"Oh, I'm into it," Jenna assures him, "but I need to work too. Tonight gives me the chance to let loose a little bit."

"Let loose, huh?" he asks. "What does that look like, Jenna?" He knows her name—they've been flirting every time he comes to the club—but they've never been together, not with her stuck outside of the events. "I'd love to see you up there, tied up with my cock in your mouth."

"You think you can hold it together down here," Jenna asks, "if I suck your cock?"

Steven glances around. No one is near, though the small hum of nearby voices is close enough. "You little vixen," Steven says.

"Of course," Jenna says, moving aside to let him sit on the stool. She crawls beneath the table, then gestures him to slide closer. Her eager hands are on his pants as soon as he is close enough, and she unzips his fly to pull his cock free. She strokes him once, twice, then warmth engulfs him as she sucks him into her mouth. Steven moans, hands slamming flat on the tabletop as he closes his eyes.

Jenna is skilled, her mouth working with her hands to get him instantly hard. Steven still has his eyes closed when a voice says, "Excuse me, sir. Is this the way to Serenade?"

Steven opens his eyes, looking across the table to see a middle-aged couple. Serenade is the bar next door, accessible through the door to his right. Steven tries to find his voice as Jenna continues her assault, not slowing at all despite hearing the question.

"It's..." Steven begins, then rallies, pointing to the door. "It's through there."

"What's up there?" the man asks as he and his wife move to the door. He points at the stairs behind Steven.

"Private party," Steven manages. Jenna's hands begin stroking his balls, and he chokes back a moan.

"Oh," the man says, turning to leave.

"Wait!" his wife exclaims, still watching Steven. She lowers her voice, leaning down. "Is that the entrance to the Honey Pot?"

He nods, not trusting himself to speak. The woman glances at her husband. "That's the place I was telling you about," she says, "the one where Luca and Maria like to go?"

"Oh," the man nods absently, then Steven sees the realization cross his face, and his head jerks back to Steven before glancing up the stairs, eyes eager. "Oh!"

"I heard there was an exclusive holiday party tonight," the woman continues quietly. "Any chance we can get in there?"

Jenna's hands squeeze Steven's balls as she deepthroats his entire cock, and his hands ball into fists. "Sold out," he gasps. "Sorry!"

"We can make it worth your while," the woman offers, a suggestive smile on her pretty face.

"Appreciate it," Steven grunts, a hand dipping below the table to grab Jenna's hair, not sure if he wants her to keep going or to stop. "But it's a closed party tonight." He decides he wants her to continue and drags her head down. Her hand squeezes his balls again and she takes in his entire length, heavenly warm suction engulfing him. "Try again at the next event," he suggests.

"We will," the man says, giving his wife a lingering look. He reaches out a hand to his wife. "Come on, dear. Let's leave this young man alone." His eyes slide over to meet Steven's and the young man is sure the older has just realized they are not the only ones in the corridor. He winks at Steven, then leads his woman through the doors to Serenade.

Steven releases the breath he's been holding, reaches down to put both hands atop Jenna's head, and drags her down. She responds without missing a beat, pulling him deep until he releases hard into her with a groan. "Damn," he breathes, watching her wipe her mouth, fix her hair, and then climb to her feet. "You are a marvel."

"Come find me at midnight," Jenna tells him. "You can see how truly marvelous I am."

10:30PM

Back upstairs, the party is in full swing, the contest "winners" adjusting to their roles. The two female servers carry special trays with a strap that wraps around their necks and two bars across the chest, both above and below their breasts, pushing them out. As patrons collect their drinks, they can tweak the exposed nipples. The male server carries a similar tray, but his strap is longer so the tray sits lower on his body, his cock resting atop the flat surface. As he delivers drinks, one woman "accidentally" spills some of her drink on him, then leans down to lick his length, collecting all of her drink before sending him on his way.

Luca stands near one occupied cage, his leather riding crop pushed through the bars to flick the bare ass of the man inside. The man jerks, his purple lace panties barely concealing the bulge of his erection, then he kneels and leans down to suck the cock of a patron on the other side of the cage. Luca watches for a time, giving encouraging whacks with the crop when the caged man needs encouragement, then heads over to the next cage where a blindfolded woman is handcuffed with her arms above her. A man has tugged her ass against the bars and is teasing her with just the tip of his cock. Luca slips the riding crop between the bars and swats her nipples. She lets out a squeal and presses her ass against the bars, seeking satisfaction from her lover.

Behind the bar, Carter is sweating as he pours drink after drink, though he maintains a steady dialogue of suggestive quips with everyone waiting. Zoey hovers nearby to supervise, not willing to abandon him completely, and a bald man stands behind her, his hands beneath her tank top and slowly slipping down into her jeans.

"No fair!" Carter bellows, watching the show. "At least lift her up so we can all see."

At her nod of consent, the man lifts Zoey onto the bar, then slides her shorts off. She looks down at her bare ass on the bar and giggles. "Pretty sure this is a health violation." Her companion leans down to bury his face in her pussy, and Zoey leans back on her elbows, eyes rolling shut. "I'm not saying anything to anyone," she moans, reaching up to press the man's head close. He looks up at her from between her thighs, a hand reaching over to squeeze her nipple through her shirt.

"Baby," Carter says, appearing next to her head, "you look parched." He lifts a shot of tequila in salute, tips it into his mouth, then leans down to share it with her in a kiss, some of the liquid spilling out of their joined mouths to run down her cheeks and chin. Zoey moans, squirming as the man licking her adds his fingers, sliding inside her in rhythm with his tongue. Carter breaks the kiss, and Zoey frowns at him, nipping his lip.

"Cheater!" she says, though it turns into a moan as her companion increases his pace. "You're supposed ... to be ... working!" The last word is a yell as she comes, pressing herself against the man.

Carter chuckles, smirking at her as he moves away to serve a gorgeous redhead who has just walked up to the bar. Zoey hops off the bar, heading over to the bench to watch a group of people playing with a woman who sits in the center, her arms bound above her head, a blindfold covering her eyes, and a cock in her mouth and another in her ass. As Zoey approaches, another man maneuvers slowly beneath her, adding his cock to the party between her legs.

On the large low table to her right, Samantha lays on her back, a man's face buried between her legs while she leisurely kisses a dark-haired woman. Zoey recognizes Emily, Ryan's wife, and she scans the crowd for Jessica's replacement tonight, spotting him next to the St. Andrews cross, helping a man tie up a woman with elaborate knots. A longer look reveals that it is Jessica who is being bound, the assistant manager naked and eager as they move from her wrists to her feet. Her hat is pulled down tight, covering her eyes. Two men stand nearby, clearly waiting for her to be restrained before moving in to play.

Zoey looks back to Samantha, enjoying the sight of her boss finally relaxing at work. A large body steps close behind her, and she glances up to see Will, the bouncer's face flushed. He has lost his t-shirt somewhere, his carved chest bare, and she presses back into him, rocking her hips against him.

"Little Zoey," Will growls, leaning down to kiss her neck. "Can I have some time tonight?"

"Definitely," Zoey tells him, hands wandering back to find the bulge of his cock through his pants. Her eyes don't leave the scene on the big table.

"Oh, I see," Will whispers, his hands sliding around to her front–one gripping her breast through the shirt while the other dips down, clever fingers finding the sweet spot between her bare legs. "You like to watch." His hand moves in a steady rhythm, his other hand massaging her hard nipple. "You think I don't see you over behind the bar every night, watching everything?"

"I see you, too," she whispers, turning her head to find his mouth. "You like to watch just as much as I do."

"I want to watch you cum," he tells her, hand moving faster between her legs as they kiss, tongues exploring as he sucks on her lips.

Zoey moans, skin flushing as the orgasm draws nearer. "Only if," she manages, speaking into his mouth, "I get to watch you cum as I ride your cock!" Her hand frees the cock in question as she shudders, but she recovers quickly, giving him a few hard pumps. Their eyes meet, and they both scan the club for a free space. With a chuckle, Will lifts her up and carries her over to the bar, setting her down on the edge on the far end, the same place the other man had laid her earlier. Zoey sees that Carter is still chatting up the redhead, but she doesn't care. Will is more than enough for her right now. Without a word, he moves between her legs, sheathing himself in one quick thrust. Zoey wraps her legs around the huge bouncer, sitting up enough to brace herself with hands on both shoulders, riding him as hard as he pounds into her. She keeps her eyes on his for the first few moments, then raises an eyebrow, bites her lip, and very slowly, pointedly, runs her eyes down his body to where they are joined, watching as he plunges into her.

"Oh yeah," he moans, "watch me fuck you."

"Fuck me, baby," she goads, moving harder now, faster, their bodies slamming together on the bar, months of sexual frustration releasing in a powerful connection.

When he is about to cum, Zoey reaches up and grabs his hair, forcing him to look down and watch her pussy engulf his cock. "Cum for me, baby!" she orders, and Tom obeys with a groan, a satisfied smirk crossing his face as he sags against her, chest heaving with exertion. "Oh, are you tired, baby?" Zoey croons. "I thought bouncers were in better shape."

At her words, Will lifts her up, spinning her around so his back leans against the bar and she still sits on his cock, her legs around his hips and her hands on his shoulders. Still holding her, he walks slowly back across the club, passing the table where the man between Samantha's legs has been replaced by Tom, the other bouncer slowly fucking the manager with measured thrusts as they kiss passionately.

"How's this for shape?" Will asks, pressing her back against the wall. He lifts her up so her pussy is even with his mouth, draping both legs over his shoulders, and holds her steady against the wall. "Now," he says, his breath teasing her sensitive skin, "tell me what you see."

Zoey giggles but looks back at the table. "Tom is fucking Samantha," she says. Will sighs. "No, little voyeur," he orders. "Tell me better than that."

Zoey grins, hands twining in Will's hair as she looks down at his gorgeous face inches from her pussy. "Tom is fucking Samantha," she repeats, "well. His ass is glorious," she continues, "all hard muscle like I imagine yours must be, and Samantha's gorgeous breasts are bouncing with every thrust."

She is rewarded with a long lick, followed by a suck. "More," he breathes into her.

"I want him to suck on her nipples," she says. "They're so big and pink. Fuck, I want to suck on them."

She gasps as Will continues to lick her, his hand moving beneath her ass, a thumb caressing the edge of her pussy.

"Oh!" she says. "Looks like Emily is back in the game–she's climbing on top of Samantha now, sitting on her face while she and Tom kiss. Her hands are massaging those breasts. I'm glad someone is."

As she narrates, another man approaches them, a tall blonde with a huge cock. He raises an eyebrow in question, and Zoey moans. "Hey Will," she says to the bouncer between her thighs, "you up for a third?"

Will abandons her pussy for a moment, twisting to look at the newcomer while still holding Zoey up against the wall. "Tobin!" Will greets the blonde. "You want some of this?" He nods at Zoey splayed open at face height, and Tobin nods, leaning in to bury his face in Zoey's pussy for a moment, learning her curves. Will adjusts so her other leg rests on Tobin's shoulder, then his hand drifts across Tobin's shoulder, moving the other man close, and Zoey looks down, one leg on each man's shoulder, and watches them kiss. Tobin reaches out to stroke Will's hard cock, then Will turns his head, returning to his work sucking Zoey's clit. His eyes close and he moans into her, clearly enjoying Tobin's touch.

"It's switch night," Tobin says, "and I want to fuck you, Will." He looks up at Zoey who nods excitedly at the prospect of another show, then turns his attention to the sexy bouncer, eyes hot with desire.

Will leaves Zoey's pussy long enough to nod at Tobin, and then they shift, Will settling back to face her directly and Tobin moving behind him, his cock already hard in his hand. He kneels, burying his face in Will's ass, and Zoey groans, cumming at the sight of the two sexy men below her. A moment later, Tobin is standing again, and Zoey watches as he pumps his cock, sliding his own pre-cum down the shaft before he presses his cock against Will's ass. The bouncer tightens for an instant, then relaxes as Tobin's hand reaches around to stroke his cock, and the hands on Zoey's thighs relax, his mouth moving slowly against her pussy as Tobin inches his way closer, easing inside Will a centimeter at a time. Zoey buries her fingers in Will's hair, jerking his head so he has to look at her.

"I want to watch you," she says, "as he fucks you." After a pause, she adds, "Describe it to me, Will. How does it feel?"

"So good," he groans, resting his cheek against her thigh.

"Not good enough," she judges. "I need more."

"His hand on my cock is moving at just the right speed," Will murmurs, eyes closing as he sinks into sensation. "That alone would be awesome, but..." His voice trails off as Tobin pushes even more, and Zoey feels the moment when he is truly inside Will, the bouncer's body shuddering in ecstasy. As Tobin begins to move, slowly at first, Will sags against the wall, still supporting Zoey, but using her and Tobin to hold him upright. "I feel him ... everywhere," Will moans. "It's everything I love about sex and more."

Zoey turns her attention to Tobin, the blonde fucking Will with more enthusiasm now, and he meets her eyes as he moves, leaning over to nibble on Will's neck, leaving red marks in the wake of his love bites.

"Room for one more?"

Zoey looks over to see that Emily has abandoned the table where Samantha and Tom are fucking again, focused on each other with an intensity that Zoey envies, but then Emily drops to her knees, sucking Will's cock into her mouth, and the bouncer shudders beneath her.

"Oh fuck," he moans, then buries his face in Zoey's pussy again, hips jerking in rhythm as Emily sucks his cock and Tobin fucks him from behind. The four of them rock in a slowly building movement, and soon Zoey shudders against Will's clever tongue. Will cums with a shout into Emily's mouth and then Tobin shudders behind the bouncer. They all pause, spent, regaining their senses, and then Emily scoots aside, Tobin steps back, and Will lowers Zoey to the floor with trembling arms.

"Now," Zoey says, "that was the athleticism I was expecting from you."

Will chuckles, turning to give Tobin a long lingering kiss, and the four of them stumble over to an unoccupied corner of the low table, Samantha and Tom noticing them long enough to scoot sideways and give them more room.

Across the room, another voice rings out. "Midnight! Switch!" Suzy is standing in front of the bar, still clothed, but the look on her face means she won't be for long. Zoey glances over to the bar, where Carter is still pouring drinks, and the big man winks at her, gesturing with the bottle in his hand.

She has a job to do, but the night is still very young. Zoey plans to celebrate the end of the year with a bang.

MORE BOOKS FROM 4 HORSEMEN PUBLICATIONS

EROTICA

ALI WHIPPE

Office Hours
Tutoring Center
Athletics
Extra Credit
Financial Aid

Bound for Release
Fetish Circuit
Now You See Him
Sexual Playground
Swingers

CHASTITY VELDT

Molly in Milwaukee
Irene in Indianapolis
Lydia in Louisville
Natasha in Nashville

Alyssa in Atlanta
Betty in Birmingham
Carrie on Campus

DALIA LANCE

My Home on Whore Island
Slumming It on Slut Street
Training of the Tramp
The Imperfect Perfection

Spring Break
72% Match
It Was Meant To Be… Or Whatever

HONEY CUMMINGS

Sleeping with Sasquatch
Cuddling with Chupacabra
Naked with New Jersey Devil
Laying with the Lady in Blue
Wanton Woman in White
Beating it with Bloody Mary
Beau and Professor Bestialora
The Goat's Gruff

Goldie and Her Three Beards
Pied Piper's Pipe
Princess Pea's Bed
Pinocchio and the Blow Up Doll
Jack's Beanstalk
Pulling Rapunzel's Hair
Curses & Crushes

NOVA EMBERS

A Game of Sales
How Marketing Beats Dick
Certified Public Alpha (CPA)
On the Job Experience
My GIF is Bigger than Your GIF

Power Play
Plugging in My USB
Hunting the White Elephant
Caution: Slippery When Wet

SHAE COON

Bound in Love
Controlling Assets

For His Own Protection
Her Broken Pieces

LGBT Erotica

Dominic N. Ashen

Steel & Thunder
Storms & Sacrifice

My Three Orc Dads: a Novella

Eskay Kabba

Hidden Love
Not So Hidden

Grayson Ace

How I Got Here
First Year Out of the Closet
You're Only a Top?
You're Only a Bottom?
I Think I'm a Serial Swiper
Lookin in All the Wrong Places

What Makes Me a Whore?
A Breach in Confidentiality
Back Door Pass
My European Adventure
An Unexpected Affair
Finding True Love

Leo Sparx

Before Alexander
Claiming Alexander
Taming Alexander

Saving Alexander
The Case of Armando

Discover more at 4HorsemenPublications.com

Other Anthologies

4HP Anthologies

Teen Angst: Mix Vol. 1
Teen Angst: Mix Vol. 2
My Wedding Date
The Offices of Supernatural Being: Office Memo 1
The Offices of Supernatural Being: Office Memo 2
The Sentient Space Log 1
The Sentient Space Log 2
Vampires in Vegas
Invoking Destiny

Demonic Anthologies

Demonic Wildlife
Demonic Household
Demonic Carnival
Demonic Classics
Demonic Vacations
Demonic Medicine
Demonic Workplace
& more to follow!

XXX- Holiday Collection

Unwrap Me
Stuffing My Stocking